Good Girl, Bad Habits

By Shaneschia Kay

GOOD GIRL, BAD HABITS
First Edition: June 2013
Copyright © 2013 by Shaneschia Kay

Universal Kingdom Print of RJTIO LLC
United States of America (USA)
Los Angeles, CA
www.universalkingdominternational.com

Affiliates:
RJTIO at www.rjtioc.burstout.net
Forever Trust Charity at www.forevertrustworld.com
BurstOut at www.burstout.net - RJTINC at
www.rjtinc.net
Universal Kingdom Print, Forever Trust Charity,
BurstOut, and RJTINC are all Divisions of RJTIO LLC.

The characters and events in this book are fictitious. Any similarity to real persons, living or dead, is coincidental and not intended by the author.

Cover Design by: Nolan Kabrich
Author Photo by: John Bennett

ISBN-13: 978-0615820347
ISBN: 0615820344
Universal Kingdom Print

Chapter 1

The rain was pouring down heavily, and the clouds covered the sky leaving no room for the sun to shine through. All I wanted to do was just lie in bed. Going to work was the last thing on my mind, especially at my dramatic ass job. It was like an episode of the "Real World" with a splash of "The Apprentice." Everyone was so intent on finding out everyone else's business while trying to use the information just to make it to the top. Some were even willing to go all the way with the head boss, who resided in Massachusetts. He added more to the drama. He would call and tell one employee that one person said something about the other, which would lead to a big argument and eventually to someone getting fired after he got tired of them calling him with the back and forth bullshit. It seemed as if someone got fired every day, and I myself had been on the verge in the past due to the whole family shit. There was a new HR director and apparently the head boss in Massachusetts said he had to let someone from our office go. He left the decision up to the new HR director as to whom she wanted to keep. At that point, to save her sister's ass, the vice president asked her to let me go and in exchange she would also assist with HR task when needed.

The tables turned when she realized that the vice president's sister could not perform any duty that was asked of her. And like that, she was gone. I think I just got lucky unlike the others. I was working in hell, but with my salary I learned to live with it.

I got out of bed, washed my face, and brushed my teeth. As I reached in the shower to turn on the water, my fiancé Jamaal crept up behind me and started licking my neck. "Chill out, Jamaal - you know mama got get ready for work," I said with a grin on my face.

"C'mon babe. My dick is hard as hell."

"No Jamaal. I'ma be late for work now move," I said shoving him to the side.

"Aight then. You wanna play hardball huh? Just wait until tonight, girl," Jamaal sang as he turned around and walked out of the bathroom.

I jumped in the shower and got dressed. In a hurry, I grabbed my bag, kissed Jamaal, and yelled for L.T. to come downstairs before he was late for school, and it was off to the everyday soap opera. Work was the usual shit. I walked in, and there was Yvette and Brenda going at each other's necks. Apparently Brenda went back and told one of the other girls some shit about Yvette's personal life. I thought that was good for her and hoped that she would learn her lesson from telling all these bitches at the job her business. I myself kept my personal life separate from work, but I guess with an office full of females that was difficult for some of them to do. Before you knew it, the boss in Massachusetts was on the line and so was someone's ass. After calling a conference with the whole office staff, Mr. Edwards threatened that if he heard any more bullshit from the two then someone would have to go. In fact, he even said that if our office kept up with the unprofessional shit, he would clear the whole office out and start over. At that point, I didn't give a damn as long as I got a few months of unemployment to get me by while I was on the search for a new job. It was obvious to me that these bitches were never gonna get their shit right. Besides, Jamaal was a technician supervisor working at a big company in Norwalk making good money.

My office phone rang and there I was running through the office, away from the gossip to answer it. "Thank you for calling Financial Inc., this is Ni'raisha speaking, how may I help you?"

"Hey girl." It was Tay on the other line.

"Hey, what's up girl?"

"You tell me. We still going out to Club Lusion tonight or you gon stay ya ass up under Jamaal and be boo-booed out?"

"What? Yeah ok. The only reason you wanna go to that damn spot anyways is so you could see Tyrone ass and flirt with other niggas in his face to try and get him mad."

"Shit, hell yeah. That nigga cheated on me with that whack ass broad so now I gotta remind him of what a good thing he had." Plus that bitch is probably gon be there too, and her bisexual ass might just be watching harder than him. Then I can tell that nigga, 'I'm so bad' ya bitch' want me?'"

I laughed. After all, she could be right. "You crazy Tay."

"Well I'm out of here at 5:30, and I'ma hit your phone so we can hit up the mall to grab something to wear for tonight. I'ma get off this phone now because who knows, these raggedy ass bitches up in here might be trynna sabotage me." Tay laughed.

"Aight girl, I'll talk to you later."

Time moved like a turtle throughout the day. In between the rain banging against the pane, the phones ringing, and all of the bickering from the girls, I was just anxious to get out of that dump.

The mall was jammed packed like a night club. For the teenagers it was the place to be on the weekend. They would all meet up in the mall to hang out and shop. I advised Tay ahead of time that we would need to hurry and get what we needed and get out. "Ooh Tay, look at that brotha right there."

"Yea okay, Jamaal will kill you and that nigga. Be stupid if you want to," Tay responded.

I laughed. "Girl Jamaal ain't gon do shit. And you act like dudes don't do the same shit we do when they out with their boys."

Tay gasped, "Yeah, you ain't neva lie."

Just then the same cutie I was staring at walked over to me. "What's good, shorty?" he said. "You looking beautiful, What's ya name?"

I looked at Tay unsure of whether to blow him off or speak. She gave me the nudge which meant, "Bitch you better say something." So I answered. "Ni'raisha, but people call me Ni."

"That's a pretty name," he replied.

"Thanks. What's your name?"

"Ronald, but you can call me yours."

I laughed even though I thought his joke was lame and played out. Then he went on to tell me how I had a beautiful smile and how he'd love to take me out someday. Tay stood to the side pretending to be window shopping but I knew her nosey ass was listening. After agreeing to give him a call, I locked his number in my phone under Ronika and walked away.

Tay looked at me and smiled. "So you gon call him?"

"No...I don't know. Ain't nothing wrong with going out to eat, Tay. It ain't like I plan on sleeping with him."

"Yeah, we'll see," said Tay.

I gave her the look that said, "Bitch stop hating," and we headed into Aldo.

I walked in the house and set my bags down. I prepared myself to go into the living room and ask Jamaal to watch L.T. for me. He would usually spend weekends at my mom's house but my mom and a friend of hers had planned a night at the casino. Although Jamaal wasn't L.T's biological father, he had always treated L.T. as if he were his own. I was sure he'd say yeah because he had become so attached to L.T. Jamaal had been in my son's life since he was seven and he was now twelve. L.T. had even started calling Jamaal "dad" because he became the person he looked up to. His biological dad was always in the streets hustling, and when he wasn't selling drugs he was either stealing or committing robberies. He eventually earned himself a permanent spot at the correctional institution, serving life. He had killed an undercover officer in a drug deal gone bad. This was behavior that I refused to let L.T. follow. He had been back and forth to jail since I had become pregnant with L.T, and I had stood by his side due to the fact that he was going to be the father of my child, but this time I had had enough. Five years had gone by, and I was still dealing with the same shit. There was no way in hell I was going to spend the rest of my life making trips up to a damn prison, or subject my child to it.

Jamaal, on the other hand, was perfect. He was the kind of man a woman would want her son to take cues from. I had met Jamaal when I was 22 years old. I had just purchased a used car a few weeks prior, and it had broken down on my way home, leaving me stranded. Jamaal pulled up on the side of me and asked if I needed a hand. That's when I learned that he was 26, a mechanic supervisor at a local shop, and had just moved to Connecticut from Atlanta a little over a year ago. He got my car started and handed me a card with his number on it. I thanked him and was on my way. I ended up calling him about a week later, and our relationship picked up from there. I was living in the projects at the time, and he was renting a small one bedroom in one of the low key sections of Bridgeport. About a year later, he had bought a house and insisted that L.T. and I move in. He couldn't help but remind me that we were now going to be a family and everything was no longer his or mine but ours. He had gotten us a nice single family, three-bedroom house with a big family room and a huge backyard in Stratford. He didn't have any children and planned on us having a family. Once we moved in together, he went to school to become a technician and made it happen. As far as I was concerned, no one could take his place. He knew L.T. loved nothing more than to stay at home with him and play video games.

I sat down on the sofa next to Jamaal. "Hey babe," I said as I kissed him on the lips. "You got any plans tonight?"

"Nah I'm chillin. Why?"

"Can you watch L.T. so that I can go out with Tay? She going through some shit and just wanted to get out of the house."

"Where Ty at?" Jamaal asked.

"Who knows?" I replied.

At that moment I think Jamaal got the point. "Go ahead and go out, I'll watch him."

"Thanks babe," I said as I got up out off the couch to give him a tight hug to express how much I appreciated it and I headed upstairs to get ready.

The line was long as hell and from the looks of things Club Lusion was jumping. The only reason Tay wanted to go to Lusion was because she knew this was Ty's spot. You could catch that nigga at Lusion every Friday rain or snow. The one thing that I liked about this club is that it was 25-and-over, which was a plus for me. I was 26 years old, and the last thing I wanted to do was hang up under a crowd of immature 18 year olds. Tay had on a pair of Seven jeans with her new cowboy boots that she had just bought from Aldo and a shirt that would make you think she might as well had come topless. I had on a pair of Levi's skinny jeans with my knee high boots and a shirt that wasn't too revealing but just enough to show a little of my cleavage. Once Tay took off her jacket, women started giving her dirty looks while the fellas, on the other hand, were giving her a different kind of dirty looks. One girl even made it her business to wait until we were walking by and then starting talking about how disgusting Tay looked in that shirt. Tay replied that she was just mad because her fat ass couldn't wear it. After letting them go back and forth for a minute, I could see that things were about to get heated so I grabbed Tay by the arm and said, "Fuck this bitch, let's go." As we walked away, all she did was yell over the crowd about what she would do, but considering the fact that she didn't swing I figured she was more than likely all bark, no bite.

Up on the next level, we spotted Ty. He looked over at us, as if he was surprised, I guess it was because Tay and I hadn't been there in months. Once they had gotten together, he gave her some story about how he didn't want her in there because niggas be bugging and if he seen a nigga in her face trynna violate then he was gonna have to hurt them. So Tay figured that she would just stay out of Lusion to avoid getting him caught up in any trouble. He had been with the chick that he was cheating on Tay with, so he turned his head back quickly so that she wouldn't notice us. She had known who Tay was, and Tay knew who she was. The streets were always talking. They'd see each other in the streets, give each other dirty looks, and keep it moving.

A cutie had come up to Tay and offered to buy her a drink, and she accepted. As she walked away with him, I could see Ty on the other side of the room trying to sneak and see what she was doing every time his chick would turn her head. I looked over at Tay, and she and her friend seem to be getting very friendly at the bar laughing and drinking, and I knew she was doing all of this in an attempt to get Ty mad. At one point, the guy even leaned over to whisper in her ear, and it almost looked like he kissed her on the neck. Since Tay seemed to be occupied at the moment, I figured I would just have one drink, so I walked over to the bar and ordered a Malibu with pineapple. Somebody was going to have to be sober enough to drive home, and it looked like that someone would have to be me.

Ty waited for the right opportunity to approach Tay. His other chick had went walking downstairs to the lower level. I could respect the fact that she wasn't trynna stalk a nigga in the club and try to force him to follow behind her every move. Had she seen "Tay," I doubt she would have left Ty alone. Ty glanced toward the stairway to make sure he was in the clear and he headed over toward Tay.

"What you doing here, and why the fuck you wearing this?" he said grabbing the front of Tay's see-through shirt. "I hope you don't think this shit is cute!"

Tay grabbed his hand off her shirt and pushed it away. "Why you so worried about what I'm doing, huh? You ain't my man, remember?"

The other guy budded in to ask if they were a couple, and Tay replied, "No. He's my ex." I guess her saying that was enough because he got up from the bar and walked away shaking his head. I walked closer to the side of the bar Tay was on because I could sense that some shit was about to go down. Ty had an I-run-shit type of attitude, and Tay had an I-don't-give-a-fuck attitude, so the two together was like pouring cooking oil on an already flaming fire. They'd just ignite. Ty was yelling at Tay, calling her a nasty bitch, and he told her that all she was good for was sucking his dick. Tay got all up in his face and started calling him all kind of names. After she called him a dirty dick nigga, I decided it was time to end this shit because not only was she embarrassing herself but me as well. As they continued to yell vulgarities back and forth at each other, I started to pull Tay away from him.

Just when I thought it was over, Ty's chick appeared in the crowd that Tay and Ty created and got all up in Ty face. "You still fucking this bitch?"

"Nah I ain't fucking dat hoe!"

"So what the fuck are you over here arguing with her about?"

As they began arguing, Tay jumped in to address the fact that she called her a bitch. Ty's chick was not about to back down from Tay. She got all up in Tay's face, and before I could grab Tay, she swung on Ty's chick. Ty was such an asshole to not even attempt to break it up. He was definitely getting some enjoyment off of them fighting over him and seemed just as entertained as the rest of the crowd. Tay was my girl, and I didn't care that she was winning; I had to jump in because this bitch had a lot of mouth. Once the bouncers broke it up and kicked us out, she promised us that we were gonna get ours, as we headed down the stairs where the exit was located. It didn't matter what she was talking about. She was the one laying on the floor bloody while her supposed-to-be man stood there and watched. It was funny that now that it was over Ty was now trying to help her up, as if he really gave a fuck. If you ask me, she should've kicked his ass for that.

On the way home, Tay was so amped up she could not help but re-enact the scene as if I had not even been there. "Bitch had my titties all out!" Tay said as she laughed. But it's all good 'cause we gave dat bitch a beatdown!" she yelled as she blasted Crime Mob's "Knuck if you Buck." I looked over her at in her seat bouncing up in down and reciting the lyrics. I smiled and shook my head. Tay had a lot of shit with her, but she was my best friend and I loved her to death. That night when I got home, Tay texted me saying that Ty called her apologizing for what happened and wanted to come and talk to her, and like a lot of foolish woman, she agreed. From the moment she told me he was coming by, I knew that meant that they would be back together. Maybe it turned him on seeing her set it on his other chick like that. I was a little pissed because not only did they just finish exposing their whole lives in the middle of a fucking club but we just beat his bitch ass which meant that I now had problems as well. I shook it off. Although I wish she would have made a different decision I knew that she could not help who she loved and as her best friend I would still have her back.

Saturday morning had arrived, and I was just thankful enough not to have to endure the drama at work. Today would just be an easygoing day for me, I decided. I cooked breakfast and called for Jamaal and L.T. to come downstairs to eat.

"So how was your night baby?" Jamaal asked.

"Well for the most part we spent more time driving to the club than we spent in the club." I joked.

"Why what happened?"

"You don't even wanna know," I sighed.

"If I didn't wanna know then I wouldn't have asked you, now would I?"

"I'll talk to you about it when you and L.T. get back from playing ball."

"Yeah aight," Jamaal said nodding.

I turned to L.T. "And how was your night, mister?"

"It was cool. Dad and I ordered pizza and played some video games. I busted his butt in Madden." L.T. laughed.

"It's all good," Jamaal replied, "'cause I'm about to bust your butt when we get out on the court." We all laughed.

"You better go easy on my baby, Jamaal."

"Ma, can we go see a movie tonight?" L.T. interrupted.

"Yeah, but just remember if the movie you pick is whack, it's coming out of your allowance."

L.T. laughed. Drinking the last of his OJ, he glanced over at Jamaal and said, "C'mon Dad, let's go play some ball so I can beat you and get it over with."

Jamaal shot him a grin. "Yeah aight, let's go.

They put on their jackets and they were off to the YMCA.

After clearing the table and washing the dishes, I called Tay to see what she was doing. "Hey Tay, what's up?"

"Nothing much girl. I'm about to get my ass up and get ready."

"Where you going?"

"Ty taking me out to brunch since he's gonna be busy for the rest of the day. He said he wanted to spend some time QT with me."

I personally thought he was full of shit. "Oh aight then, go ahead and enjoy yourself and call me when you get back."

"Aight Ni."

"Oh and Tay."

"Yeah girl?"

"Don't forget your blade."

"Girl, I'm good, I got this."

"Aight, I'll talk to you later."

I couldn't stand the idea of Tay still being with Ty, but it was her life, and I knew Tay would do what Tay wanted to do.

I had just gotten out of the shower and put on my clothes. I turned on the television and decided to try and catch up on the latest news when the phone rang. It was Natty. Natty was me and Tay's friend from high school. We had formed out little clique, and the three of us had been tight since. She was the first of the three to luck up. She had met Mark while we were in high school. He was a few years older than her and already in college. By the time she hit college, she was only able to obtain her associates in business because she had gotten pregnant with her first born, Tishaya. Mark decided that he did not want her to work and preferred for her to be a stay-at-home mom, although she wanted to further her education and obtain her bachelor's degree. They had a big single family house in Trumbull and he had even gotten them a beach house for the summer. Anyone from the outside looking in would assume that they had the perfect family.

"What's going on with you?" she said. "Are you going out tonight?"

"No not tonight. Tonight is family night girl. Me, Jamaal and L.T. are going to the movies. You should have caught me yesterday. Me and Tay went to Lusion."

"Oh god," Natty replied. "Was Ty there?"

"Yeah, he was there with this sideline ho all up in Tay's shit. He was hating on her hard, but we ended up beating this chick's ass, and by the end of the night Tay and Ty were back together."

"Are you serious?" Natty replied. "Tay needs to realize that she can do better than that sorry ass nigga."

"She will eventually. Everyone has to go through shit to learn their lesson. Right now she is so blinded by Ty's sweet talk that she don't even mind the hustling and going through all the drama bullshit, but trust me she'll get fed up sooner or later."

"Well I hope so."

After catching up on what was going on with Natty and her life in the past week since I had last spoken to her, I advised her of the day and time we would be getting together to get fitted for my wedding, and she agreed. I told her that I would call her sometime throughout the week so that we can come up with something to do for the following weekend.

Jamaal and L.T. came barging in, sweating from playing ball.

"So who won?" I asked. "C'mon now, you know that's a stupid question, baby. Need I remind you about that mean jump shot I got?" Jamaal said as he pretended to shoot a basket.

"I let him win 'cause I felt bad about the beating I gave him in Madden yesterday," L.T. grinned. "Oh ok," I smiled, "now go get your little sweaty self in the shower and then come eat."

"Aight." L.T. replied as he headed upstairs.

"So what happened last night baby?" Jamaal said grabbing the pitcher of cold water out of the fridge. After giving him the rundown of Friday night's events, he slammed the pitcher of cold water down on the kitchen table. His facial expression showed that he did not approve of my behavior. "Look baby, I know Tay is your homegirl, but she knows how Ty is. She already knows how he gets down and if she's going to accept it then so be it but you not gonna be out there fighting with her. You got L.T. to worry about, and I refuse to let anything happen to you over your homegirl's bullshit. I don't have no problem with Tay, she cool, but I do have a problem with her trynna involve you in her shit. She don't care about being in the streets fighting 'cause she ain't got no kids and no job. You do."

In a way I knew what Jamaal was saying made sense. In the past year, Tay and I had been in several fights, and none of which were mine. She had even been cut in the face once but that didn't stop her. Jamaal was right. Maybe I would sit down and have a talk with her to try and get her on the right track. After all, she was my best friend, and I would hate for anything to happen to her. Besides, if she found a job she might find it difficult to find time to party all the time.

Chapter 2

Our third movie night of the month had approached, and we had gone to see "Shrek in 3D." Afterward, we headed to Applebee's to grab a bite to eat. While we were eating, we were able to catch up on what L.T. was up to at school and the latest adventures at my job. Then we talked a little more about the wedding. Jamaal and I still hadn't agreed where we would go for our honeymoon, so we asked L.T. where he think would be a great place for us to go. I wanted to go to Cabo san Lucas, and Jamaal wanted to go to Jamaica. Since we could not come to an agreement, Jamaal and I decided to take L.T's advice and take a three-night four-day cruise to the Bahamas. Our wedding date was set for June, so we were sure cruising in the summer time would turn out wonderful. I still couldn't believe that in just a few months I would be Mrs. Richardson. I was lucky to have Jamaal in my life. He was there for me when I needed him, and he never judged me. That was just the kind of man I needed. Natty was married, I was due to get married, and now hopefully Tay would meet the right one and get married. Although I supported her decisions, I just hoped the man she chose to marry wouldn't be Ty's sorry ass.

When Sunday arrived, the thought of having to go to work was driving me insane. I was so happy to have this Sunday to just relax. We had dropped L.T. off at my mom's house after dinner Saturday night, and Jamaal was at a friend's house watching the game. This would be a day just for me – no man, no kids, and I definitely wasn't cooking dinner. I was in the living room watching TV when the phone rang.

It was Tay. What's up Ni, guess what girl?"

"What? Wait let me guess. You beat somebody's ass today?"

Tay laughed. "Hell no. Not today. I got good news today."

"Oh if you got good news then I definitely wanna hear it."

Tay laughed. "Anyways, Ty got one of his boys to hook me up with a job."

"Congratulations! So where are you going to be working at?"

"I'ma be working at Kitties as a dancer."

"What? Uh uh Tay. You tripping."

"Ty said I could make some good money, and shit girl, if I got the body then why not use it? Ya dig. Besides, we about to move in together in two weeks, and I'ma need my own money. You know Tay don't believe in depending on no nigga to hold her down. If shit don't go right, at least I'll still have my own dough to make moves. Shit, I'm tired of living off the state and being shacked up in this small-ass rooming house, and that little chump change Ty be giving me ain't shit."

"I could understand you being frustrated about your money issues, Tay, but why don't you just go and find your ass a regular job and stop trynna sell yourself short?"

"Look Ni, this is where the money is at. Yo, I went up in there yesterday to try it out and I made close to $500. Shit, Ty boy said that's not even what they consider a busy night there. Shit, it will take a week to earn that at a regular job, and I'm just trynna get this money and live right."

"And you call that living right, Tay?"

"Oh God, here we go. Ni, why can't you just be happy for me instead of always being so negative?"

"Ummm, maybe because I know that you're better than this, Tay, but if this is what you wanna do then I support you and congratulations. Just make sure that you doing this for you and not for no nigga."

"Thanks girl," Tay responded. She no longer seemed excited.

I attempted to change the subject. So what you up to today?"

"Nothing. Just waiting for Ty to come over. He's gonna bring some movies over, and we're gonna order out. I'm about to get my groove on, and then I'ma catch me a little nap before work tonight."

"Oooooh that sounds like a plan girl," I said trying to lighten up the mood. "Well you go ahead and do you and I'ma catch up on the soaps."

"Aight Ni, I'll talk to you later."

"Oh and Tay?"

"Yes Ni?"

"Make the money, don't let the money make you," I said as I laughed.

Tay laughed, too. "Bye Ni." Click.

I hung up the phone and took a deep breath. I picked up the remote and turned up the television. Thank god for Soap Net because things were getting heated on "One Life to Live." There was nothing like seeing Jessica be crazy with her alter egos. After the soaps had gone off, I flipped through the channels to see what else was on. "Snapped" seemed to be the next best thing on the television. I was amazed at how many women killed men for money that they never even got the chance to spend.

For some reason that I could not understand, the fine young brother that I had met at the mall popped into my head. I was not interested in anything more than a friendship with Ron, but I did wonder what kind of guy he was. A friendship with Ron was very possible as long as he accepted the fact that I was engaged. I picked up my cell phone and scrolled down to his number. I started to have second thoughts about calling him; after all, I was engaged to Jamaal and knew that he wouldn't approve of it but on the other hand Ron seemed like a cool guy. I would just call him for a little friendly conversation and would be sure to mention Jamaal so that I would avoid sending any mixed messages. I exhaled and pressed talk.

"Hello."

"Hello Ronald."

"Who is this?"

"This is Ni. I met you the other day at the mall."

"Oh yeah, what's good sexy?" I thought you was trynna neglect a nigga."

I laughed. "No. I just been a little busy."

"Busy doing what, going out with your little girlfriends, huh? It's gonna be kind of hard for them to keep you warm at night."

"No actually I don't get out much. I have a son, so a lot of my weekends consist of spending them with him."

"Oh well that's cool." Ron responded. "So where he at now?"

"He's at his grandmother's house."

"So what you doing in the crib?"

"Just relaxing and watching TV."

"You wanna go grab something to eat?"

Even though I should've objected to this, I didn't. The thought of his sexy lips and his muscular build had me believing this was the right thing to do. We would just go and grab something to eat, and that would give me an opportunity to tell him about Jamaal, the love of my life. "Sounds good," I said.

"Aight. So meet me at the Olive Garden in about an hour," Ron said.

"Cool" I replied.

I jumped up out of the recliner and began singing check up on it while imitating one of Beyoncé's moves. Then I picked up the phone to call Jamaal.

"Hey babe," he said. "What you doing?"

"Nothing, chillin. Watching the game. What you doing?"

"About to go over to Tay's house for a little while. We're gonna have a drink to celebrate her new gig."

"I thought you was staying in today," Jamaal said.

"I was until Tay called me bugging me about coming over and having a drink with her to celebrate. So I told her I would have a drink with her so she can stop hassling me." I laughed.

"So Tay got a job?"

"Yep," I said failing to mention what type of job it was. "Make sure you have a drink for me," Jamaal said jokingly.

"Alright baby, I'll talk to you later."

"Aight." Click.

I raced upstairs to get dressed. While heading out the door I gave Tay a ring. After calling her three times in which she didn't answer, Tay finally picked up. "What's up Ni?"

"Tay, I'm going out for a bite to eat with the guy I met at the mall, but I told Jamaal that I was going to your house to have a drink to celebrate your new job. I'm not gonna be able to answer my phone, so I need you to look out. Just in case he should call your phone, tell him I'm in the bathroom and text my phone. I will go in the bathroom and give him a call back."

"Ni, are you fucking crazy?"

"What Tay!"

"What? Bitch, you are engaged! You acting like you forgot how crazy Jamaal ass is."

"Tay it's nothing serious. I'm just going out to eat."

"Aight Ni. But if this shit fall back on you don't say I didn't warn ya black ass."

"Alright, alright, Tay, I gotta go bye." Click.

Ronald looked so fly in his Timberland boots and his baggy jeans. He had the clean shave and a fresh shape up. His cornrows hung down to his shoulder and his caramel complexion made him all the more sexier. His sexy lips resembled L.L Cool J's, and that just turned me on even more.

"Hey sexy, how you doing?" he said as he approached me with open arms.

"I'm good," I said hugging him back.

"Damn, you looking good girl, he said admiring my Seven jeans.

"You don't look so bad yourself, I replied.

He pulled my chair out, and I sat down. We briefly looked over the menu that the waitress had brought us and placed our order.

"So what's a beautiful woman like you doing single?" Ronald asked.

"Well actually Ronald–"

"Ron," he corrected me.

"Ron, I said. I'm not single."

"What? So you gotta man?"

"I have a fiancé."

"So what you doing out with me then?"

"I ain't doing nothing wrong."

"Yeah aight," Ron said as he took a sip of the glass of water the waitress had placed in front of him. "You think your man will see it that way?"

I smiled. "Well, that's why he doesn't know."

"Come here," he said, gesturing for me to lean toward him. Ron met me halfway. "I'ma take you from him," he whispered in my ear.

I smiled but deep down inside, I knew that that would be an impossible task. Our dinner conversation was very innocent. We discussed our children. He had an eight-year-old daughter named Tiffany who lived in Rhode Island with her mother, so he would only see her a couple a times a month. He was a hustler but eventually hoped to get on his feet and get a real job so that he could obtain custody of his daughter. According to him, his baby mother was no better than him. She was in a relationship with a drug dealer whom he didn't have any intentions of getting to know. He was supposedly abusive and disrespectful, and Ron stressed that he could not have his daughter around that. Ron went on to tell me that he was single. After dinner and an interesting conversation, we gave each other a goodbye hug, and I headed home.

When I got home, Jamaal and L.T. were already there. Jamaal had did me the favor of picking L.T. up from my mom's house. He was just such a perfect man. I loved the fact that I never had to ask him to do things for me. He would sometimes inconvenience himself just to please me. I started to feel guilty for my "behind the scenes" dinner with Ron.

"Did you enjoy yourself at Tay's?" he said.

"Yeah. Me, Natty and Tay had a few drinks and did a little bit of girl talk."

"So where's ya girl gonna be working at?"

"She got a job a

s a dancer," I said trying not to be precise.

"I'm guessing you not talking ballet," Jamaal said.

I chuckled.

"Yo, your girl is crazy. I'm glad I got me a good girl," Jamaal said as he crept up behind me and wrapped his arms around my waist. "Just don't surprise me and have me walking up in no strip club and see your ass on a pole."

I nudged him lightly in the stomach with my elbow. "Shut up Jamaal."

"Nah but for real, you really need to talk to your friend. The way she living her life is foul, Ni."

"Jamaal, I tried to talk to her, but she insists on stripping. She said that the money is good, and her and Ty are trynna make moves."

Jamaal smirked. "I don't think Tay realizes how unstable her life has been with this dude in it."

"I know. But this is something she is gonna have to see for herself."

"Yeah, she will," Jamaal said as he headed upstairs to the shower.

The day went by faster than expected. Our local office consisted of ten women, and it was nothing more than a miracle that three members of the gossip crew were out. Tanya and Shari worked in sales, so they were traveling for the day and Marie had taken her vacation so she wouldn't be returning for a week. Considering she was the leader of the gossip gang, I was even more relieved to have her nosey ass out of the office. The work week was more easy-going for that very reason. The rest of the gossip crew spent the week kissing ass. They weren't so tough without their leader, but we knew that was a temporary phony phase that would soon be over once Marie returned. Of course, there was still a little tension in the air, but no one was fired yet, which was a good sign.

The work week flew by, and finally Friday had come, and although it had been much more easy-going week, just being in the atmosphere made me sick to my stomach. I was thankful for every Friday that came along and freed me from all the drama and phony bitches at the job. I would spend time with Jamaal and L.T. that night, and then I would go out to J's on Saturday. J's was the local bar in Bridgeport, and I liked that it was never really crowded. A lot of the people that came to J's were older. J's was the type of place that you can jam to the oldies as well as the recent generation of music. People were always on the dance floor, drinking, dancing, and enjoying themselves. There was hardly ever any drama, which was more so the reason why I liked it. Of course, Tay voted on going clubbing, but Natty and I voted against it. It was okay to go clubbing once in a while, but I wasn't about to make it a habit. Natty was married with two children and jumped at every chance she got to get out of the house. Her husband Mark was a lawyer and had his own law firm, so he would work long nights most of the time. The only time they really got to spend together was on Sundays and that was if Mark was lucky enough to catch a break with work.

That Saturday night, I was just and excited to get out with the girls for a little while. Although I hate to admit it, Ron has been on my mind this week. Just thinking about his body turned me on. That's the one thing I had to admit that he had over Jamaal, but I had to remind myself that I was engaged, and I had to stop thinking these crazy thoughts. My thoughts were interrupted when I heard L.T. yelling, "Ma, are you almost ready?" Brian and his mom are waiting for me. She's taking us to the Entertainment Arcade and then out for pizza."

"Okay baby I'm coming," I replied.

L.T. enjoyed spending some weekends with my mom but said he did not feel like playing Bingo, as my mom would always beat him anyways. Since we spent Friday together, no one seemed to really mind going their own ways. L.T. had wanted to stay over a friend's house so Jamaal and I decided we'd each get out and do something with our friends and next Saturday would be our time to catch up for family night. I enjoyed Saturday nights with my family because it gave us a chance to catch up on things that took place during our week at work and L.T's week at school.

"Jamaal, have you decided where you going yet? I asked.

"Yeah, me and the guys are gonna go shoot some pool and have a few drinks at Drew's Pool in Norwalk."

"Oh, ok," I replied. "That sounds good."

"So what you up to for the night?"

"Oh me, Tay, and Natty gonna go down to J's and have some drinks."

"Oh I see how ya'll do - ya'll going to go try and pick up some old men," Jamaal joked.

I smiled. "Whatever Jamaal."

"Don't be letting Tay try and have you up on the club scene every weekend. You know how she get down."

"Ma!" L.T. yelled from the front door."

"I love you baby and I'll see you later," I said to Jamaal while picking up my keys from the kitchen table.

"I love you, too."

Chapter 3

J's was on fire that night. The DJ was off the hook and everyone seemed to be enjoying themselves. There were some people on the floor getting down to the Cupid shuffle, and me, Tay, and Natty joined in. The DJ even took it back to Slick Rick and Mary J's real love. We danced a little longer, and then we walked over to the bar and ordered seconds. I ordered a Malibu with pineapple, Natty ordered a Long Island Iced Tea, and Tay ordered a Sex on the Beach. Go figure. The room was getting hot, and we decided to go sit down and cool off so we grabbed a table.

"So how's the job going, Tay?" I asked.

"Oh girl, can't you tell? I got this new Michael Kors handbag!"

I laughed.

"Where the hell you working at, Tay?" Natty asked.

"Ty got me a job at this spot called Kitties in Stamford."

"What! Tay are you serious? Now girl, you know you can do better than that."

"Look, Natty, don't start judging me. I'm cool with my job, and I make more than enough to pay my bills. I enjoy what I do, and besides, Ty only had my best interest in mind. That's the reason he don't got me working in Bridgeport."

I laughed. "Tay you say it like Bridgeport is all the way in South Carolina somewhere. It's only like twenty to thirty minutes from Stamford."

"It's a small world," said Natty.

"Look can we just get off the subject 'cause I don't speak about nobody else's situation," she said looking at me with her face frowned up.

"What situation?" "Natty asked.

"She went out to dinner with this guy she met at the mall last week," Tay said with a smile on her face.

"What! Is this true, Ni?" Natty asked, as she looked over at me.

"Yeah but it wasn't even like that, so Tay stop trynna hype it up to be more than what it was."

"You know you ain't right for that, Ni," Natty said.

"That's what I told her," said Tay.

"No you didn't," I replied.

"Okay but I did say you was crazy–"

Natty interrupted. "Ni, Jamaal is good to you and when you got a good man you need to appreciate him. You ain't even married and you already committing adultery," she joked. But for real, Ni, it's hard to find a good man so you better get your priorities together. If you're gonna be having infidelity now, and you're not even married yet, then what's the point of moving forward?"

I replied, "Ain't nobody cheating on Jamaal. Ya'll are acting like I slept with him."

Tay just couldn't resist giving her input. "Yeah Ni, but if you keep dealing with this nigga, who's to say what might happen? You really need to let it go now before someone gets hurt."

As much as I wanted to tell them how he was on my mind earlier, I decided against it seeing that they were against me.

"Look ya'll, Natty said. I wasn't gonna say anything, but ya'll my girls so I'ma keep it real with ya'll. I think that Mark is having an affair."

"What would make you ask that?" I asked.

"Over the past few months he's become so secretive about his phone conversations, for one. For two, I been getting hang up calls at home, and he didn't even come home last night."

"Well did you ask him if he was messing around?" Tay asked.

"Yeah but he just denied it. He didn't even give me a reason why he didn't come home last night. The only thing that he gave me an answer for was the phone conversations and even that was full of shit."

"Well what did he say about the phone calls?" I asked.

"All he said was that he be on important business calls, so he has to go somewhere private to take them."

"And what did he say about the hang up calls?"

"He said that it was probably just telemarketing calls or someone with the wrong number."

"Oh, that's the lamest excuse I heard in a while," said Tay.

"That's why I'm telling you, Ni, you got a good man and you need to hold on to him," said Natty.

"I will. But you don't worry yourself about Mark. If he wants to act a fool and not realize what a good thing he has, then so be it, but he still gotta take care of them kids regardless."

"Shit, he probably feel like he can do shit 'cause he's the breadwinner," said Tay.

"Well, it was his idea for me to stay at home and care for the kids. I cook, I clean, I take care of the kids, and do everything that a wife is supposed to do."

"Just look at it this way, if Mr. Mark the lawyer does fuck up, you could divorce his ass and get the cash," Tay joked.

"And you still got your associates in business, "I reminded her.

Natty exhaled. "I know ya'll, I know."

Just then Neyo's "Ms. Independent" came on. "Oooh this is my song," Tay said getting up from the table. "C'mon ya'll, let's hit the dance floor."

I looked at Natty, "You gonna be alright girl. Now c'mon let's go and shake our asses."

We made our way to the dance floor, and all of the issues that just lie in front of us moments earlier were now behind us.

I woke up on Sunday morning with thoughts of how much fun I had the night before. It's been a while since the three of us hung out in the night life together. The one thing that me, Tay and Natty knew how to do was turn a party out, and that was exactly what we did. I laughed to myself and headed downstairs to make breakfast. Lucky for me, Jamaal had already done me the honor of making breakfast. I sat down with him and began eating.

"How was your night?" Jamaal said as he sat at the table drinking a cup freshly brewed coffee.

"It was good, I replied. "Me, Tay, and Natty caught up on some gossip. Then we had a few drinks and got on the dance floor. That's what's up, Jamaal. And how was your night, boo?" I asked as I leaned over and kissed him.

"Me and the fellas had a few drinks, shot some pool, and watched a little sports TV at the pool hall."

"Oh alright," I replied.

"And guess who was there?"

"Who baby?" "Mark."

"Oh really?" I frowned.

"Yeah. Are him and Natty separated or something?"

"No. Why?"

"Look babe. It's none of our business what goes on in Natty and Mark's marriage so what we're discussing doesn't leave this house aight?"

"Aight."

"I'm dead serious, Ni."

"I said alright, Jamaal," I said raising my voice.

"Mark was with another chick."

"Oh was he?" I asked.

"Hell yeah. He walked in with his arms around her waist, and could you believe the nigga had a nerve to walk up to me and introduce her like she was wifey?"

"Oh, he can't be serious," I said. "Natty stays at home playing her part as a wife and he gonna go and cheat on her for another bitch."

"Well what's done in the dark will come to the light," said Jamaal.

At that moment, an idea popped into my head. Although I knew I should have minded my business, Natty was one of my closest friends, and it wouldn't be right for me to know something about her husband's infidelity and not tell her. At the same time, I had to keep my loyalty to Jamaal. So instead of actually telling her, I would do her one better. I would help her catch his no good ass in the act. We would follow him. Then hopefully she would leave his cheating ass while he'd leave half his income along with her. I would have to keep this a secret from Jamaal because I knew that he would not agree with the whole ordeal.

"Baby," Jamaal interrupted my thought. "Are you gonna eat the rest of your bacon?"

"No," I said pushing my plate toward him. "You can have it." The thought of Mark trynna run game on my girl made my stomach turned.

"I'm gonna go pick L.T. up and do a little shopping. You wanna roll with me?"

"No, I'm good baby. I'm still a little worn out from last night. I'm just gonna stay in and relax today. You know tomorrow it's back to the Bad Girls Club for me."

Jamaal laughed. "Aight then, your loss." Jamaal got up from the table and headed to the bathroom to get ready.

I picked up the phone and called Natty. The phone rang at least six times and then went to voicemail. I sat down in the recliner and kicked my feet. The phone rang. It was Natty calling back. "Damn girl, what you up to that you couldn't answer the phone?"

"I was in the kitchen fixing Mark some breakfast. He gon tell me not to pick up my phone until his plate was in front of him. You know he think he runs shit."

"Shit, he got a lot of nerve," I replied. "You better get his ass in check, Natty; you ain't his damn slave."

"I know," she replied. "Where's Jamaal?"

"He's in the bathroom getting ready to head to my parents' house and pick up L.T. and then do some shopping."

"Oh okay. What time did he get home last night?"

"He got home before me. He was already in bed when I came in, why?"

"Mark told me that he bumped into Jamaal at the pool hall and they hung out until about three, but he didn't get in the house until a little after four in the morning. It don't take no damn hour to drive from Norwalk to Bridgeport, and if Jamaal was home when you got in, then Mark is definitely lying to me-"

"Hold on Tay," I interrupted Natty.

Jamaal walked into the living room. He landed a kiss on my lips, "I'll be back in a few hours baby."

"Alright," I replied kissing him again.

Jamaal grabbed his keys and headed out the door. I lifted the telephone receiver back up to my ear. "Okay now what were you saying?"

"Ni, Mark said that he was with Jamaal until about three In the morning but that was a lie because you said Jamaal was already home when you got there. We left J's at two o clock, and it damn sure didn't take either of us two hours to get home."

"Of course he's lying, Natty. When we left J's, I walked in my house at about 2:30, and Jamaal was laying in the bed watching TV. I don't know where the hell Mark was at or what he was doing, but the one thing I know for sure is that my fiancé was home in bed when I walked in this house."

"That's what the fuck I'm saying, Ni. The nigga is doing me wrong, and he's trynna play me for a damn fool," Natty said with anger in her voice.

I saw this as an opportunity to pitch my idea to her. "Shit, if you really wanna find out what the fuck Mark is up to, we can always play private investigators and follow his ass around."

"I had thought about hiring a private investigator when I first became suspicious, but if I go into the account to take money to pay a private investigator, he's gonna want to know where the money went. He pays close attention to his money."

"His money! Girl, you are his wife and you have his kids so it's as much as your money as it is his!"

"Yeah, I know. But I'd rather avoid the drama with him."

"Well shit. There's no need to waste money anyways for something we can do ourselves. This is what we're gonna do. We're are officially conducting our own investigation. Are you down or what?"

"Yeah, I'm with it," Natty responded.

"Cool. I get off work at five o'clock on Friday and so we could probably meet up at Tay's crib. I just have to give her a call to confirm but you know that chick don't object to drama."

Natty chuckled. "Alright, well I hope our mission turns out successful. I'll drop Tishaya and Mark Jr. at my mom's house when they get out of school Friday."

"Alright and I'm gonna call Tay and let her know what's going on so we can set this plan in motion."

"Okay. Just call me and confirm with me if we are still on."

"Alright, I replied. Oh and Natty please tell me you got an extra key to his car in case we have to repossess his shit."

Natty laughed. "Yeah girl, unbeknownst to him but I got that."

"Cool. So I'll give you a call Friday afternoon sometime you just get your childcare straight with your mom."

"Okay," Natty replied. "I will talk to you on Friday."

As soon as I hung up the phone with Natty, I picked up the phone to call Tay on her cell, but I got her voicemail so I left her a message to call me back. I started flipping through the channels on the television when my cell phone rang. It was Ron. I was a little confused because we had agreed that due to my situation he would not call me and instead I would call him. I forwarded him to voicemail but after careful consideration decided it was probably a good idea to call him back so that he wouldn't keep attempting to call me back. It would be just my luck for him to call and Jamaal answered my phone. Jamaal and I had nothing to hide in our relationship, so not only did we leave our phones around each other but if my cell phone had rang and I couldn't make it to the phone then he would answer it, yet more reason why I didn't approve of Ron breaking the rules. It would be mighty strange for me to all of a sudden, start carrying my cell phone around the house with me everywhere I went and I knew Jamaal would become suspicious. I was now having regrets about not blocking my number out when I called him but it was too late to dwell on it now. "What's done is done," I mumbled to myself as I scrolled to my recent calls and pressed talk.

The phone rang twice before Ron picked up. "What's up sexy?"

"I thought we had an agreement that I would call you. You know, I have a fiancé."

"Damn, I can't even get a hello or how you doing first? You just gon call me flipping out?"

I giggled. "Hi, how are you doing?"

"I'm good and yourself?"

"I'm fine."

"I apologize for calling your phone, but I hadn't spoken to you since I saw you last week. I got worried."

"Yeah okay," I replied.

"Nah but on the real I was thinking about you so I just wanted to give you a call to see what you was up to."

"I'm chilling, and what's good with you?"

"Nothing much. Just trynna get rich or die trying," he laughed.

Although I knew that Ron's way of making money should've turned me off, I couldn't help but be turned on by this hood mentality. He was living life in the fast lane, and it was keeping him fly.

"So what you doing today ma?" he said.

"Just relaxing. I gotta go back to work tomorrow, and it's more than likely going to be a hell of a work week."

"Can I see you today?"

I knew that it might not have been a good idea to agree to see him. I was physically attracted to him and did not want things to go any further than they already had. "Actually, I think I'm just going to relax today. I have to cook dinner before my son and my fiancé gets home."

"Well do you think I could possibly see you next weekend?"

I paused, unsure of what to say.

"Is that a no?"

"I don't know, Ron. I don't think that it's a good idea. I'm engaged, and this just doesn't-"

Ron interrupted. "Ni, it's not like we having sex or nothing. We're just two friends hanging out, chilling. I like you but I accept the fact that your engaged, and I'm not trynna do anything to mess up your happy home. I promise I'll behave aight? So what you think?"

After taking a few seconds to think it over, I accepted his offer.

"Aight so just give me a call this week, and we'll figure out what day we gonna get up."

"Alright, I said. I will talk to you soon."

"Aight sexy."

I pressed the end button and sat my phone down on the living room table. "Damn, why am I doing getting involved with this drug dealing thug when I got an honest hardworking man at home," I asked myself. I started thinking the next time I saw Ron should probably be the last. I needed to tell him that maybe it was best if we didn't see each other anymore. I was definitely going to end this before someone got hurt.

The phone rang, and Tay was on the other end crying. I knew that now was not the right time to tell her about the plan to catch Mark cheating. "Tay what's wrong?"

"This nigga got the nerve to be fucking with that sleazy trick again." I knew that she was referring to Ty.

"And how do you know this?"

"Because I called his phone to see when he was coming by because I was going to cook dinner for him and the bitch answered his phone! She said that her and Ty were still fucking and that he's been staying with her except for the two nights he had told her he had stayed at his mom's crib which was a fucking lie because he was with me! He came by my job the other night and told me that he wasn't gonna make it over because he was gonna be on the block all night to try and get this money so that we can move into our place next week but his little sorry ass was lying about that, too!"

"Are you serious?"

"Yep," she answered. I told her that we were moving in together, and she said that Ty had told her that his mom was having some hard times so he was going to be moving in with her to help her out with her bills."

"Oh no he didn't," I said.

"Oh yes the fuck he did," Tay replied.

"So what are you gonna do now?"

"I don't know. I love him but it's only so much a woman can take? I hate that bitch so much, Ni. I told her that I'ma fuck her up when I see her."

"Now hold up, Tay. You can't blame that chick for Ty's actions. She probably feeling the same way you feel about her. He's the one who led you on so you need to be beating his ass, not hers."

"But I know that no good hoe knew he had a girl before she slept with him. Everybody in the hood knew he was my man."

"Tay, whether she knew it or not, that's beside the point. You're not her homegirl or nothing, therefore she had no loyalty to you. She don't owe you shit 'cause she don't rock with you, Tay. Ty is the one who caused all of this drama, not you and her."

"Yeah okay, Ni, but this chick's mouth is reckless. She came at me crazy on the phone talking about what she was gonna do to me when she see me and how Ty is her man and-"

"Tay," I interrupted her. "What does this sound like to you, because it sounds to me like a bunch of childish bullshit. Ya'll are going back and forth talking about what ya'll are gonna do to each other and Ty's probably sitting back, smoking a blunt and laughing at both of ya'll assess.

The question that remains is what are you gonna do?"

"I don't know, Ni. I didn't even get a chance to speak to Ty yet because that fucking bird hung up on me."

"Tay, but what does it matter that she hung up on you? She answered his phone so you know that he was definitely with her. Anything else is irrelevant."

"I know but I love him. It's hard starting over Ni. I don't wanna do this shit again!" She started crying even harder.

"Tay look you know I support you in everything you do but if you only been with Ty for a year and a half and your already going through this, then just imagine what else is to come."

Tay took a few seconds to take in what I said. "You're right. I don't know how much more of this I can take. I need to let this nigga go. I'm done and he better not call anymore with his deceitful ass."

"Do you have to work tonight?" I asked Tay.

"Yeah, she replied.

"Well then you need to get some rest. Go take a nap and give me a call when you get up. And stop stressing yourself out over Ty. God has a plan for you trust me girl."

"Alright," Tay replied. "Thanks for being a good friend."

"You're welcome; now get you some rest and I will talk to you later."

"Alright." Click.

After hanging up with Tay, I walked into the kitchen and grabbed the ground beef out of the freezer and set it in the sink to defrost. I looked up at the ceiling and thanked God for sending me a good man.

Chapter 4

Thursday afternoon had been pretty easygoing, and all of my work for the day had been completed. I was surfing the web looking at wedding gowns when my office phone rang. "Good afternoon, this is Ni'raisha speaking."

"What's up girl?" Tay cut me off.

"Tay, why you always calling my office phone instead of calling my cell?"

"Ummm 'cause you never answer your dam cell phone when you at work."

I laughed. "I'm sorry I didn't call you back on Sunday night. I woke up and was running late for work. Girl this late night work has just been killing me."

"I hear you," I replied.

"Ty stopped by my job Monday night."

"Um, and what did he say?"

"He admitted that he was fucking with her again."

I said in my head, "Gee ya think?"

"But he really wants to make things work this time and he said he knows that he can better man. He made it clear to me that he would rather leave her than lose me."

"And you believed him?"

"Ni, people can change, and I know he's trying. He's been staying with me since Monday night when I got off of work. When I go to work he's there, and when I come home, he's there."

"So I take it ya'll back together?"

"Yeah but it's gonna work this time, Ni. I can feel it. We're moving into our apartment on Saturday and we're going to the furniture store today to pick out our new furniture."

"And whose name is on the lease?" I asked.

"Mine. Ty didn't wanna put his name on anything that might draw attention to him."

I thought that was a plus for her. At least she didn't have to worry about him trynna kick her out on the streets. "Well no matter what, you're my girl, Tay, and you know I stand I'ma back you 100 percent." I filled Tay in on the details regarding Natty's situation and the plan. Tay was eager and pissed off at the same time and couldn't wait for Friday. She promised if she caught Mark with another bitch, she was gonna beat her down and that Natty could consider it an early Christmas present. Once again I had to remind her that the chick was not to blame. She accepted my reminder and changed her mind about delivering an old fashion ass whooping to Mark's mistress.

"So just call me tomorrow, Ni, and let me know what time we're gonna meet up. And it better not be too late 'cause I gotta be to work at 10:30 tomorrow night."

"As of now, we should be meeting up at about 5:30. Let me just confirm with Natty and we can all meet up at your house."

"Aight cool. Just call me when you confirm."

"Okay Talk to you later, Ni."

I decided to give Ron a call to set up a time to meet up for Friday night. I felt that if I didn't call him back, he would call me. It would probably be a good idea to meet up with him and let him know that we can no longer see each other. This would also give me an opportunity to see his sexy ass for the last time. After talking on the phone with Ron for about five minutes, I heard drama erupting in the office and decided to end the call but not before we setting a time to meet up at nine o'clock on Friday. I would have to tell Jamaal that Natty and I would be hanging out for a few. I had to get this over and done with. I walked out of my office and right into the line of fire. Once again, dramatic ass Marie was having it out with one of the girls. Shari had overheard Marie talking shit about her to one of the other gossip girls, and she approached her to let her know that she didn't approve of it. Marie went ballistic and started yelling at Shari about how she didn't know how to do her job and she was mad because her man wanted her. She ranted on about how he tried to get with her outside in the parking lot one day when he had just came out of the building from seeing her. Marie was such a drama queen not to mention a bitch. It was sometimes hard to understand the words she was speaking because her English was still a little off, but she knew just enough English to get under someone's skin. And when she was really fired up, she would make her way over to a couple of her Hispanic friends and start speaking Spanish, but somehow the conversation would always get back to the individual. Then her punk ass would get shook up when she was confronted and deny having said anything. She would then start pointing fingers, which only caused more drama. She hadn't come at me wrong, yet and if the day came where she had, it would be a day she would regret. Shari on the other hand was cool. Although I never shared any of my business with any of them, I liked Shari. She would look out for me when I had to make little runs during work hours. When the president would call for me and Shari answered the phone, she would either tell him that I was in the bathroom or out for lunch, even though I had already taken my lunch break. She would call my cell phone to advise me of his call so that I can return his call. Marie and her gossiping ass crew would just tell him that I wasn't there and that they didn't know where I was so when I did speak to him there was always an explanation needed.

I grabbed Shari and bought her into my office. "Calm down, Shari. Why are you letting that dumb ass bitch get to you?"

"I'm just sick of that bitch coming at me. She's been saying slick shit out of her mouth for a while now, and I've been letting it slide.

Then she goes and calls Mr. Edwards, and he always takes her side. I think she be sucking his dick or something."

I laughed. And no sooner than she said that there was a knock on my office door. Mr. Edwards was on the phone and wanted to speak with Shari. As Shari walked away, I grabbed her and reminded her that no matter what we were at work and she needed to keep it professional and joked that she could kick Marie's ass after work hours.

Marie had called and told Mr. Edwards about their dispute, but according to her Shari had blown a conversation that had nothing to do with her out of proportion. I felt like kicking her pathetic lying ass my damn self. As expected, Mr. Edwards sided with Marie and turned all of the blame on Shari. He said that Shari was an adult and needed to let go of the he-said-she-said shit. He demanded she got her act together and this would be her final warning. This had not been the first time Shari and Marie had gotten into a verbal altercation and not once had she been the one to start it. I was sure that a few of Marie's crew being in her office with her when she had made the call, had also helped her win this one but another thing I started considering was that maybe Shari was right. Maybe Marie was creeping with Mr. Edwards. He was married, but it was known that he had messed around with a few of the younger women in

Massachusetts so what would make her different? After all, she did do a lot of traveling to Massachusetts for so called business meetings for the company. Besides, this is probably what she considered "working her way to the top." Mr. Edwards had not even given Shari the chance to tell her side of the story. She walked away with anger in her eyes and came into my office to let me know that if she ended up losing her job behind Marie's shit, she was going to whoop her ass before she goes. I agreed. Mari deserved anything that was coming to her conniving ass.

When Friday finally arrived, I couldn't wait for the clock to hit so that I could get out of the hell hole, especially since I would be on vacation until the following week. After Thursday's episode, I would have thought that Marie would have learned her lesson, but she resumed her usual gossip sessions. I had to remind myself that It was kind of hard to learn a lesson if you're not being chastised for your actions. If she can go to work and start drama without being fired than why not take advantage of it? I only hoped that she could back up all of that talk should Shari have to lay that ass whooping on her. I grabbed a cup of coffee from the kitchen and headed back into my office closing the door behind me. I picked up the phone and placed a call to Natty and Tay to confirm a time to meet up for our mission.

At 6:30 in the evening, Natty, Tay and I were parked in the parking lot of Mark's law office. We settled on taking Tay's 2003 Hyundai Sonata because Mark had never seen Tay's new car and the fact that she had tinted windows lessened our chances of being spotted by him. Mark usually was out of his office by 6:30, but he had a habit of working late and that was exactly what he had called to tell Natty. According to him, he was up to his shoulders in paperwork, and this would be one those nights where he would be working again.

"Oh, guess who I bumped into today?" said Tay.

"Who?" I asked.

"Ty's ex girl."

"What she say?" Natty asked.

"That chick didn't want it. I was with Tisha, and you know she be ready to get down and dirty, but the bitch was quiet as kept. She was talking all that shit about how she better not catch me slipping and what she was gonna do but she was all shook up. She couldn't even look me in the face."

"You just better play it safe because I don't trust that chick," said Natty. "Everybody in the hood know that bitch is up to no good."

"Please, I ain't stunting that chick. She know the deal. She knows my name ring bells in these streets, and that's why her ass was scared. I don't know why she's all obsessed with Ty anyways. She was only fucking with him for four-and-half months."

"Now Tay how do you know that he was only fucking with her for four-and-a-half months?"

"Because Ty told me. The girl is a fucking stalker, and she need to get over it. She be blowing his phone up trynna get back with him and she's hating 'cause Ty don't want her ass."

"And how can you be so sure that he's not still fucking her?" Natty asked.

"'Cause he ain't got time for no other chick. He's on his grind most of the time, and when I get in from work he's home. He's been on the right path the past few days since we got back together. Every night he's been coming home to mama." Tay laughed.

"Ain't that Mark right there, Natty?"

"Yeah that's his ass," Natty replied as she slid down in her seat. "Follow him Tay."

We followed Mark from his law office in Fairfield to the west end of Bridgeport.

"Who the fuck lives over here?" Natty said aloud.

"Bitch, you tell us, it's your man," Tay joked.

"Shut the hell up, Tay, this is serious; now stop playing," I said.

Mark pulled up into the parking lot of an apartment complex. He parked and exited the car.

"Park over there Tay," I said pointing toward an empty parking space in the back of the parking lot.

"I feel like I work for the FBI," Tay whispered.

I looked over at Natty. "Could you really imagine Tay not saying something that's not crazy?"

Natty shook her head, "Hell no."

"Oh Natty, don't act like you don't be saying crazy shit," Tay said.

"Nothing that amounts up to the shit you say," Natty responded.

"Shhh, there they go," I said. Mark emerged from the house with a short, thin woman. She had a caramel complexion and wore a long blonde shoulder-length weave.

"I wonder if he paid for that," said Tay. I looked at Tay with a look in my eyes that told her to shut the fuck up.

As Natty attempted to open the door, Tay pushed the automatic lock button and locked the doors. "Nah, chill Natty. Let's see what their up to first."

"Up to! As if seeing another bitch on my husband's arm is not enough to say he's creeping!"

"It's not, bitch. She's one his clients for all we know. You haven't seen them hugged up or kissing yet. Now just calm down and fall back so that when he does slip up, he can't have no excuses 'cause you seen it with your own eyes. Don't trip girl, we gonna get his ass."

At that point, Natty was even more hyped. "Alright well," she turned to Tay, "then drive bitch, follow his ass!"

I loved my friend dearly and as much as I had wanted to see her beat Mark up, we were on his mistress's property and chances were that we would very well have ended up behind bars. "Just try and relax," I said despite knowing that it was an impossible thing for her to do at the time.

At 7:30 in the evening, Mark and his mistress were inside of Red Lobster eating. We could see through the visible glass and they really seemed to be enjoying themselves. They were laughing and kissing. Tay pulled out her digital camera, rolled the window down halfway, and started to take pictures. "Girl we are going to print these pictures out so you can use them against his ass in court," she said.

It took a lot to hold Natty back but I refused to let her walk up in there and make of fool of herself. At 8:15, they were out of the door and getting back into Mark's car. I considered calling Ron to tell him I would be running late but reconsidered after remembering that I hadn't told Tay and Natty about me hanging out with him that night. The clock was pushing 9 o'clock when Mark walked his mistress to her front door, kissed her on the lips, and headed back to his 2007 Mercedes. Natty grabbed her metal bat from the floor of the car and quickly hopped out of the car. She charged toward the car with her bat raised. Mark noticed Natty and started to walk toward her, asking her what she was doing. Mark's mistress watched from her front door in shock as Mark chased Natty around the car trying to take the bat from her. Natty made her way to the front end of the car and busted out the right headlight.

"What the hell do you think you're doing?" Mark yelled as he stood focused at the busted headlight.

Natty ran around the car busting out every window.

"You are a fucking crazy bitch!" Mark yelled. "Get the hell away from my car before I call the cops!" Mark was all up in Natty's face.

She looked at him with hurt in her eyes and tears were rolling down her cheeks, "I'll see you in court," she said. She walked away and got into Tay's car dropping the bat on the floor.

"That's my bitch!" Tay yelled as she sped out of the parking lot.

"Not right now Tay." I said. I glanced over at Natty, who was crying even harder. She had her hands over her face and seemed as if reality had just kicked in that this had really happened.

"I can't believe Mark would do this to me," she said. "These last nine years of my life have been nothing more than a joke to him. We have a family and what am I supposed to tell my children? He's my husband!"

"Sweetie, just because you have kids by a man don't mean he's gonna stick by you or be faithful. But if you're gonna separate from Mark then just be cordial for your children."

"Nah, fuck that! I'm glad you fucked his whip up, and you should've fucked his ass up, too!"

"Shut up Tay," I interrupted. "Now Natty, you go home and deal with this situation, but just don't have all that drama in front of Tishaya and Mark Jr."

"I know" she said wiping the tears from her eyes. "I'm gonna leave them at my mother's house for the weekend, and I'm gonna go stay in a hotel for the night. Tomorrow I'm gonna go and pick up our clothes and then Monday morning I'm going to see a divorce lawyer."

"Girl, why are you leaving the house? He's the one that fucked up so he should be leaving."

"No. I wanna go. I don't want any memories of anything that took place in that house. I just wanna start over. Tay, can you try and get those pictures out for me this weekend so that I can take them with me when I go see this lawyer?"

"You know I got you, Natty."

We dropped Natty off to her car and gave her goodbye hugs.

"You're gonna be alright," I assured Natty as I rubbed her back. Go and get some rest and call me tomorrow. I'm on vacation next week so if you need me to go with you, I'm available."

"Thanks Ni, I'll talk to you later," Natty said.

I knew that it would not only be a long but a sleepless night for her.

The clock on the dashboard read twenty minutes after nine when Tay and I pulled up to my house. I rushed inside to take a shower and get dressed. Jamaal was at a friend's house, and L.T. would be spending another weekend with my mom. She was going to be taking him on a shopping outing on Saturday, and L.T. never denied an invitation for new clothes. When I got out of the shower and checked my phone, I had two missed calls and a text from Ron asking where I was at and advising me that he had been expecting my call over forty minutes ago. I text Ron apologizing and letting him know that I was running late but would be heading out in a few minutes.

Rather than respond to my text, Ron called my phone. "So I see you running on black people time huh?"

"Yep. Unfortunately I had to take care of some business and I didn't expect it to take that long."

"Oh aight. Where's ya man? Oh excuse me, your fiancé."

I laughed. "My fiancé is not home at the moment."

"So where you wanna meet me at?" he asked.

I suggested the AMF bowling alley in Orange.

Ron laughed. "Oh you trynna stay out of the port, huh? You think your fiancé might find out you was chillin with me?"

"Whatever. So I'll meet you there in about twenty minutes. Is that okay?"

"Yeah aight," Ron said. Click.

I laughed at the thought of Ron's jokes, but he was right. The bowling alley in Orange would be a good idea because it was not too far out of Bridgeport, but it lessened my chances of being seen by someone that Jamaal knew. I arrived at the bowling alley first and waited in my car for Ron to arrive. He pulled up moments later and I got out of my car to approach him. When I walked up to Ron, he greeted me with a hug, and as expected he was looking fresh to death. We headed inside, got some bowling shoes, and started bowling. We had a few drinks and things started to heat up a bit. Every time I was up to bowl Ron would get behind me to assist me on aiming the ball in the right direction. When his phone rang, he would walk off to take his calls, and I couldn't be sure whether it was business or pleasure. He told me that he had not been seeing anyone during one of our previous conversations, but either way it didn't matter to me. I wouldn't be seeing him anymore after tonight anyways, I told myself.

After bowling, we sat in Ron's car and talked a little more now. We briefly talked about my life with Jamaal and L.T., and then Ron told me about his past relationship. He told me about his eight-year-old daughter and how he was thankful for every chance he got to see her. He explained to me how he ended up in the streets hustling at age sixteen. His father had killed his mother in a jealous rage and then committed suicide. His 18-year-old brother had been taking care of him until he had gotten caught up in the system just a year and a half later. He had been serving a double homicide on some guys that had beat him for some drugs. His aunt had taken him in when his brother got locked up but his obscene behavior caused her to kick him out on the streets. He had been kicked out of school for bringing a knife to school and even locked up in juvenile detention for running with the wrong crowd. Once his aunt kicked him out, he went to stay with his best friend whose mom felt pity for him. She had been in a relationship with a big-time drug dealer named Rock. Rock earned his respect in the streets of Bridgeport. He told Ron that if he was going to be living with them, he would have to get a hustle to help out with the bills, so Ron turned to him for work, and ever since Ron had the game on lock. The only difference now was that Ron answered to no one. He was his own boss and everybody knew it. I could tell he was getting money just by looking at him. His gear was tight, his shoe game was tight, and his jewelry game was even tighter.

Midnight had came and gone, and I needed to be heading home. I didn't want Jamaal to start getting suspicious, especially since he had trusted me so much. Ron walked me to my car, and I stopped at the door. "Ron?"

"What's good, sexy?"

"I don't think we should see each other anymore. Don't get me wrong, you're cool, and I enjoy talking with you, but I'm getting married in a few months and this feels wrong."

"Word? That's how you feel?"

"Yes. I just don't want things to go any further because I find myself kind of feeling you and enjoying the time we spend together."

He smiled. "Aight, if that's what you want I'll get off your back then."

"Thanks," I said as I wrapped my arms around his neck to give him a friendly hug. He grabbed my face and began kissing me, and I exchanged the favor. My phone started to ring, and I pushed Ron away and checked to see who was calling me. It was Jamaal. I lifted my finger to my lips signaling for Ron to keep quiet and answered the phone. "Hey baby."

"Hey. Where you at?"

"I'm on my way home, I'm just about to leave Tay's house."

Ron looked at me smiling and shaking his head.

"Oh, Ms. Tay ain't stripping tonight?" Jamaal joked.

I said what came to mind. "No, she took the night off because she wasn't feeling too well so she asked me to come over to keep her company until Ty got home."

"Well tell that nutcase that I said hi and hurry up and get ya ass home girl, I'm waiting for you."

I got the point. He was ready to get it on. "Aight baby, I'll see you in a few," I said.

"I love you babe," Jamaal said.

"I love you too," I replied. Click.

Ron had this smirk on his face like he was hating.

"I gotta go but I hope that you understand my decision," I said to Ron as I got into my car."

"No, it's all good, I understand," Ron said. "But anyways congratulations on your engagement, and I wish you all the best." He grabbed my hand. "If things don't go right between you and your fiancé you know my number. Hopefully I'll still be single." He kissed me on the top of my hand and started to walk away.

"Alright. Take care," I said as I unlocked my car door. I watched him as he headed to his

2010 Chevy Impala, and I pulled out of my parking spot.

On my way home, I found myself daydreaming about him. I actually enjoyed the kiss we shared, but I would have to keep that to myself for now. It wasn't the right to time to tell Tay and most definitely not Natty considering the situation she was dealing with. When I got home and walked upstairs to the bedroom, Jamaal was waiting for me with the lights out and a few lit candles. I took a shower and slipped on my lingerie. I laid down on the bed, and Jamaal got out on top of me and started licking on my neck. He worked his way down to my inner thighs and started pleasuring me until I climaxed. He entered slowly, stroking me in a way that was sure to please me. Although Jamaal's sex was pleasurable, I couldn't help but to think about Ron. He was a cool person, and I started thinking it might not be such a bad idea to just keep him as a cordial friend. Then I asked myself, "What are you thinking?" That could never happen because Jamaal would never approve. Besides, I was feeling him a little too much, so it was probably best for me to stay away from him. My thoughts were interrupted by Jamaal as he called out my name while releasing himself into me. Jamaal then kissed me on the lips and rolled over to go to sleep. I turned over on my side and began to daydream until I fell asleep.

Chapter 5

The phone rang; it was Natty. "Good afternoon, Ni."

"What's up Natty?"

"I know we were supposed to meet up tomorrow to get our dresses for the wedding situated, but do you think it would be possible to reschedule? I'm just so stressed out right now, and I'm still trying to take all of this in."

"Natty, don't worry about it. I already called and set a date two weeks from now for that. You just do what you need to do to get yourself back on track."

"Do you know that when I went to the house yesterday to get a few things to bring with me back to the hotel, he came in the house screaming about how crazy I was and that he should have me arrested for fucking up his car. He was yelling about how much it was going to cost him to get it fixed, and I asked him if he realized what it was going to take to fix my life."

"And what did he say?"

"He didn't have an answer. He told me that he had only been seeing this girl for a few months now and that he never intended to fall in love with her. He said that he's in love with her and that he knows that we are going to get a divorce, but he wanted to know if there was any way can settle out of court. He told me that I can keep the house and that he would give me $3000 a month to help out with the kids."

"So all he thinking about you is not taking all his money at this point? He's not even attempting to try and get you back?"

"No and I told him that I was not settling out of court and that he deserved everything that came to him." Natty broke down crying. "Why me Ni? I don't cheat, and all I do is stay home cooking, cleaning and caring for our children. I've had opportunities presented to me in the past, but I would never jeopardize my marriage."

"I know," I said. "But what goes around, comes around."

"And do you know what else he had the nerve to say to me? He told me that what he did shouldn't matter as long as me and the kids were being taken care of."

"No he didn't!"

"Yes he did," Natty replied. "I guess that since he's the one with the job, I'm obligated to put up with his shit but it was his idea for me not to work. I have an associate's degree, I could've easily went out and got a job, Ni. He asked me to stay home and play the housewife. It was never my decision. I wanted to work."

"Well did you tell him that, Natty?"

"I told him that I wanted to work but he always wants to control shit. I guess he didn't feel like a man if he wasn't in control at all times. I wanted things to work, Ni. Mark and I have been together since I was nineteen and I couldn't see myself with no one else. All of the signs were there and I just can't understand why the hell I didn't see this shit months ago."

"We live and we learn Natty, that's life. But no matter what you do, never let him see you stressing because it'll only make him feel stronger and in control. Don't give him the satisfaction of seeing you down and depressed because that will let him know that he won. I personally think you should have said fuck what he was talking about and put the kids in school. You should've went and got yourself a job to let Mark know that although the two of you were married, you were still an independent woman and capable of holding it down on your own."

"Yeah, well I know that now," said Natty.

"If you let a man run your life then you'll always be nothing more than a follower so I'm telling you girl, do what you gotta do to gain that independence."

"I took a look at his cell phone bill on my laptop, and he made a call at 6:24 to this number. That was just a few minutes prior to him leaving his office, and I believe that it might be his mistress' number. I thought about calling it last night to find out if it was, but I realized that it doesn't matter anymore. What's done is done and like he said this is the person he wants to be with, not me."

"Natty, Normally I would tell you not to waste your time calling her, but I don't think it would hurt to give her a call just to find out if she knew that he was a married man but that is totally up to you to decide."

Natty took a deep breath, "I might just give her a call, but if she try to get it fucked up then I might just have to kick that ass."

I laughed. "Well we will cross that bridge when we get to it. I will talk to you later."

"Okay, Ni, and if it's not too much to ask, will you still be able to come with me to see this lawyer?"

"Of course I'll go with you, Natty."

"Alright thanks, Ni. I will talk to you later."

"Alright Natty." Click.

Jamaal was in the bedroom watching the television. I walked upstairs and plopped down on the bed next to him. I wasn't quite ready to tell him that Natty and Mark were separating, feeling that if I did he might automatically suspect me of telling. "So what do you wanna do today?" I asked.

"I don't know that's up to you."

"Well since L.T's not home we can probably go to the bar to have some drinks and play pool. You should call up Tay, Natty and the guys and see if they wanna get together tonight."

I immediately became nervous knowing that I couldn't call Natty. I had to come up with an excuse and quick. "Tay has to work tonight so she won't be able to make it."

"And what about Natty and Mark?" he asked.

"I was thinking that maybe we could do something alone tonight," I said.

Jamaal paused. "Let's do it then."

I took a small sigh of relief. "Alright. Did you want me to cook dinner for today or did you wanna eat out?"

"No, we can eat out tonight; I'm dying for some of those baby back ribs from Chili's anyway," he said rubbing his stomach.

"Okay," I said as I jumped up from the bed. "I'm gonna go and get in the shower."

"I'll meet you in there," he said smiling.

Jamaal and I were at the dinner table when my phone rang. I looked down at it and it was Ron. I was starting to believe that his intentions were to get me caught up so that we might have a chance.

"Who's that baby?" Jamaal asked.

"Natty," I replied looking up at him. I forwarded the call. "I'll call her back."

"So did you figure out where you're gonna get your wedding dress from?" he asked.

"Well I was browsing online and I saw a few dresses that I liked. I saw this beautiful dress online at David's Bridal that I wanted to see in person. Me, Tay and Natty are going to check out some dresses the following week."

"Well you just better get that figured out Ni 'cause we don't got no time to waste," he joked.

"It don't take seven months to find a wedding dress, Jamaal."

"Yeah but it'll soon be December," he replied.

"Jamaal, we still have two and a half weeks before the first of December and June is months away. You're overreacting." I smiled.

"I just want everything to be perfect Ni."

"I know, baby, and they will be. Let's just focus on getting through the holidays for now." '

"What are doing for Thanksgiving this year?"

"Well my mom and dad wanted us to come over to their house, but if you wanna stay home, I'm cool with making Thanksgiving dinner."

"Nah we could go to your mom's house. That should be cool. Maybe we can just make a dish to bring over."

"Sounds like a plan," I said. "Is your brother coming down?"

"No but he'll be down for Christmas."

"Oh okay," I said. "Maybe we can all go out."

"Maybe," he said lifting his fork to his mouth. "If Tay wasn't so damn hood I wouldn't have mind putting her on with my brother, but that will never work. Besides, I wouldn't want her getting my brother caught up in no bullshit with Ty."

I agreed.

After we finished with dinner, we went to B's to have some drinks and shoot some pool. It felt good to finally have a night out alone with my husband and I was enjoying every minute of it.

As soon as we walked into the house, the phone rang and it was Tay.

"I'm going upstairs to watch TV," Jamaal said.

"I'll be up there when I get off the phone with Tay," I said. "What's up Tay?"

"I just got off the phone with Natty, and she told me about Mark. She need to get his ass for all he's got. Me and Ty been through our shit, but he ain't never try to play me when it comes down to my money. He's just straight up whack."

"Natty's gonna be okay though. She's a strong minded individual."

"I hope so, Ni."

"So how are things going with you and Ty?"

"We straight. We moved in to our place yesterday and I made him change his number too. I told him if we're gonna do it, we gotta do it right."

"I hear that," I said.

"Well let me get back to work now. Gotta go shake my ass and get this money."

I laughed. "I'll talk to you later." Click.

When I got upstairs, Jamaal was already undressed and in bed. I undressed and laid with him and watched television until we fell asleep.

Chapter 6

It was early December, and Natty had been holding up a little better than she had in the previous weeks, so I decided it would be a good time to go and pick out our dresses after putting it off numerous times. Things were looking good for us. Natty had found a job as an executive assistant at a financing company and had rented a three-bedroom not too far from me. Although the job at the financing company was not exactly where she wanted to be, it was a start toward her independence and a new life. Tay and Ty's relationship was holding up, and I hadn't spoken to Ron since our last interaction at the bowling alley. Mark was still residing in the house that they had in Trumbull but had moved his mistress in, which Natty eventually accepted.

Tay and I pulled up in front of Natty's house and blew the horn. Natty looked good and was surprisingly holding herself together well. She got in the back seat of my 2007 Nissan Maxima and immediately got down to gossiping.

"So Ni, remember the time I had told you about Mark's mistress and how she had claimed she didn't know he was married?"

"Yeah," I replied looking at her through my rearview mirror. "I found out the bitch was lying. Mark's sister told me that she had gone to Mark's office to visit him one day and his mistress was there. She asked Mark in front of her how me and the kids were doing and she said that our wedding picture was sitting upright on Mark's desk. I kind of figured her ass was lying because I couldn't understand why she would even wanna be with him and move in with him after finding out some shit like that."

"Wow. He must have really worked his magic on that chick," I said. "And I would have really worked me some magic in her ass," said Tay. "It's okay cause we have to go to court in January, and I'll show his ass. He thinks he's gonna give me $3000 a month and make this all go away. Shit, I want $4000, and we're gonna set up visitation, but for now he has to come to my house and see the kids 'cause I don't want them around that bitch."

"Well how did you explain the separation to the kids?" I asked.

"I called my mom and told her about the situation the night it happened, so when I went to pick up the kids that Sunday, I sat them down and told them that me and Mark have decided to move into separate houses, but I'll still be there mommy and Mark will always be their daddy."

"And how did they take it?" I asked.

"Well not too good at first but it's going on two months now so they're handling the situation better."

"Well that's good," I said.

As we pulled up in the parking lot of David's Bridal, we couldn't help but admire all of the dresses that hung in the window. When we entered the store, Natty's face turned to a look of hurt. I didn't want her to realize that I had caught her facial expression, so I quickly turned my head. Within an hour we had our dresses picked out. I know there's the saying that you're not supposed to wear white if you're not a virgin but I figured, it's a new decade who really follows that tradition anymore? Besides, it was one of the most beautiful dresses I had ever seen. Natty and Tay would wear pretty lavender color dresses. Afterward, we stopped at Subway to grab a bite to eat and then I dropped Tay and Natty off and headed home.

When I walked in the house, Jamaal was sitting at the table with his arms crossed looking directly at me.

"Where's L.T.?" I asked. "I dropped him off to his friend's house for a little while," Jamaal said.

"What's wrong with you?" I asked.

Jamaal looked up at me. "Why the fuck did you go and tell Natty about Mark being at the pool hall with another chick?"

"I didn't tell Natty that Mark was at the pool hall with another chick!" I said being very defensive.

"Oh really?" Because I bumped into him at the gas station today and he asked me if I mentioned anything to you about the night at the pool hall. He said that ya'll followed him to that chick's house and Natty busted the windows out of his car. So when were you going to tell me that, huh? Are we keeping secrets now?"

"Ain't nobody keeping secrets from you, Jamaal. First of all, Mark had already told Natty that he was at the pool hall. She just called me to verify that he was with you because that was what he told her, and I told her that it was a lie. I told her that you were in already in bed when I got home and that was it. I never mentioned anything about no other chick."

"Okay Tay, so why does Mark seem to think that it was your idea to follow him? He also feels that the fact that I told you is how all this shit got started up in the first place. I can't disagree with him on that."

"Well it wasn't my idea, and I only told Natty what I told you I did!" I yelled.

"Well you should've just minded your damn business! That's what I think!"

I grabbed my bag and keys from the kitchen table and stormed out of the house.

I was driving around trying to clear my head. My cell phone rang, and it was Jamaal. I forwarded him to my voicemail. I was so angry inside. I couldn't believe that he would even talk to me like that. It had been a while since we had an escalated argument, and we had been getting along just fine. I knew that I may have over reacted a bit, but I guess it was because I was so use to Jamaal allowing me to control how our arguments ended. My phone beeped alerting me of a new voice message. I was not in the mood to hear anything from him and especially at the moment. I scrolled through my contact list and found Ron's number. I pressed the talk button not caring that it was probably not the best thing to do.

"Hey stranger – haven't heard from you in a while," he said as soon as he picked up the phone.

"Hi. How are you?" I asked.

"Well, I'm good now that I heard your voice. What's up wit you?"

"Nothing much. Just leaving my homegirl's house," I lied.

"Oh so you outside right now?"

"Yeah. I just wanted to call you and see how you were doing."

"I'm good, but I'm a little surprised considering the fact that I haven't talked to you in almost two months. How are things going with you and your fiancé?"

"Good, I said. "And how are you and your girl doing?"

"I don't have no girl. I was trynna get you, but you're taken."

It felt good to laugh a little.

"So can you come by and see me for a little while or do you gotta get home?"

I took a second to think about it. "I can come and check you but only for a few minutes because I have to pick my son up from his friend's house."

"I'm cool with that," Ron said.

"What's your address?" I asked. After Ron had given me his address I assured him that I was on my way and we ended our call.

When I had arrived at Ron's house I called his phone to let him know that I was outside. "Come inside," he said.

I checked my hair and made sure my lip gloss was popping before getting out of the car. I walked up to the house and took a minute to take in my surroundings. It was actually rather quiet. Ron opened the door and greeted me with a hug and a kiss on the lips. Ooh, he turned me on and once again I returned the favor. Once we stepped inside, he gave me a tour, and I was rather surprised at how neat his apartment had been. When Jamaal and I had first hooked up and I seen his place it was just as I had expected, a mess. He had invited me into the living room where "Smoking Aces" had been playing on his 50-inch plasma screen television. It was one of my favorite movies. Alicia Keys was that chick in that movie. About a half-hour into our conversation, my phone rang. It was Jamaal calling again. I quickly forwarded him to voicemail. No sooner than me forwarding Jamaal's call than my phone rang again. This time it was Tay calling.

"Could you excuse me for one minute?" I said to Ron as I got up from the couch. I walked into a small walkway that led into the kitchen. "What's up Tay?"

"Ni, he did it again."

"Who did what again?" I asked confused.

"Ty. I just called his phone to find out what he wanted for dinner, and that bitch answered the phone again."

"Damn that's crazy. Listen, you just chill out. I'm on my way to get L.T, but I'ma call you back when I get home so we can talk about this."

"Alright," she said with strain in her voice. Click.

I looked at the time on my watch. I walked over to Ron. "I have to get going so I can go and pick up my son."

"Awww. You leaving me already?" he said as he stood up and grabbed my hand. He leaned over toward me and started kissing me. He slowly pushed me down on the couch and started to caress my breast. I wanted to tell him to stop before we went the extra mile but while my mind was telling me no, my body was saying otherwise. He licked my neck as he began to unbutton my pants. I suddenly had a change of heart. I pushed him off of me and I jumped up and buttoned my pants.

"I have to go," I told him as I grabbed my bag and headed out the door.

"Call me," Ron yelled.

"I will," I said as I glanced over my shoulder back at him with a smile on my face.

On my way home, I thought about how I really enjoyed the short time I was able to spend with Ron. He had really brightened up my day. "Maybe it wouldn't be so bad to hang out with him more often," I told myself as I drove off.

When L.T. and I walked into the house Jamaal asked him how his day was and after L.T. shared the details with him, he headed upstairs to get showered and ready for school the following day. "Ni where were you?"

"I had to go for a drive to and get my mind right," I replied.

"For two and half hours?" he asked.

"Well I had to pick L.T. up, too."

"Yeah but it didn't take you two hours to pick him up, Ni. So what? I suppose you gonna try and tell me that you was at Tay's house now, huh?"

"No. I'm not gonna tell you I was at Tay house because I wasn't," I said.

"Yeah, I know you wasn't 'cause she had called the house phone for you. And why didn't you answer your phone when I called Ni? What the hell were you so busy doing that you couldn't answer my call?"

"I told you, I just needed to clear my head."

"Yeah okay," he said as he turned away and made his way upstairs. I took a deep breath and walked into the living room. I sat down and pressed the icon to check my voice message. There was a message from Jamaal. He said that he wanted to apologize for the way he overreacted. He said that he loved me and if he had to argue with any woman in this world he would rather it be me. He made it clear that he did not want anyone else. I just wished I would have listened to his message before I went to see Ron, but in my mind I had already screwed up, and If Jamaal ever found out about me hanging out with him, he would never accept it. I knew our relationship would probably be over. I hung up the phone and picked up the house phone to call Tay back as promised.

Tay sounded as if she had been sleeping. "Hello," she said.

"Hey girl. Are you okay?" I asked.

"No, but I will be. I just don't understand why I can't be enough for him. Why does he always have to have more?"

"Maybe he feels like he's the man when has two women fighting over him and all of his boys see him going back and forth between the two of you."

"But it's not right for him to keep playing with my emotions like this. If I knew where that bitch lived, I would go and fuck both of them up."

"What did she say when she answered the phone?"

"She had to answer the phone talking about 'Mrs. Michaels speaking.' The bitch was trynna be funny 'cause that's Ty last name."

"Oh she's a petty chick," I said. "So what are you gonna do if he comes crawling back?"

"Oh it's not a matter of if he comes crawling back, it's when, and that was the final straw, Ni. I'm done with this bullshit. After I hung up with you earlier, I called Natty, and we talked on the phone for about a half hour. I realized that if she can start over then so can I."

"Yeah okay," I said. "We both know damn well you ain't going nowhere. Besides, you work at his boys strip club so that's just the easy way for him to come and see you when he's ready to kiss and make up."

"I'm quitting," Tay said.

"Tay please. You're not leaving your job, and you damn sure ain't leaving Ty."

"Ni, I'm serious. Enough is enough, and it's time for me to get my life together. I've been running around with no good drug dealing thugs all my life and that's why I will never be happy because all they care about is money, cars, and hoes."

"Jay Z ain't never lie," I added.

"I was stripping not only for the money but because I thought I could keep him and please his ass as long as I had a job. Now it's time to please me Ni. I'm not going back to Kitties or back to Ty's sorry ass. I've decided that I'm gonna get a real job this time, and hopefully I will meet a real man with a real job. Shit, don't no real man respect no stripper and ain't no real man gonna want me if I'm out there stripping."

I was surprised. In all of the years that I had known Tay, I never heard her talk like this before. Maybe she was waking up after all.

"And you know what else, Ni? On second thought, I would love to go over there and beat the hell out of both of them, but it's so not worth it. I don't wanna live like this anymore. I don't wanna be 30 years old and still running around fighting just to try and maintain my reputation."

God was I happy to hear her say that. "So does that mean we won't be delivering any more beatdowns?" I asked jokingly.

"Nope, not unless it's necessary. And..."

"And what?"

"First thing tomorrow morning, I'm going to look for me a job."

I laughed. "Oh okay. I ain't even mad at you. But Tay, if you're serious about changing your life then I'm happy for you. You just remember that you have to stay strong because this will be a challenge for you. God has put each and every one of us to a test to see how we handle it and he will forgive us for our sins. Once he sees you making an effort, he will assist you on your journey." I said this knowing that I should be the last person preaching right about now.

"I know, that's right," said Tay. "That's why I'm gonna avoid him and any negative situations as much as possible. Oh and I'm changing my number tomorrow so I'ma call you with my new number."

"Oh wow. You really ain't playing," I said.

"Nope. And as soon as I get a job, I'm gonna move so he won't know where I live. My lease is a month to month so that's a plus."

"I'm just glad that you're making moves, but keep in mind that for you to make changes, you are going to need an attitude adjustment girl."

"I know, and I'm going to work on that." I yawned. "Well let me get off this phone and get my ass in the bed for work tomorrow."

"Alright, I'll call you tomorrow Ni."

"Okay girl. Stay positive."

"I will," Tay replied. "I'll talk to you later." Click.

I headed upstairs to the shower and then to the bedroom to try and smooth things out with Jamaal. Unfortunately, he had already decided to fall asleep, so I decided to do the same. I had such a crazy day, and Monday was sure to be the same.

Monday morning had arrived and the work day was moving slow. I sat at my desk and surfed the net as I usually did when there wasn't much work to do. I was still a little upset about the argument with Jamaal the night before and just hoped that no one got on my bad side for their sake. I appreciated Jamaal's attempt to settle the argument with his message apologizing for his behavior but I still wasn't over the fact that he had even come at me the way he did. On the other hand, I had really enjoyed myself with Ron and he always looked his best when I saw him. I picked up my phone and texted him asking him how his day was going and a few minutes later he texted me back telling me that he was having an okay day and asking me what I would be doing for the weekend. I replied that I would be busy on Friday and Sunday but should be available Saturday night. We set a date back at his house for Saturday, and then I went back to surfing the net.

We had been five hours into the workday and work had started to pick up. The phones were ringing heavy and out front had been crowded with people waiting to apply for loans. I didn't mind us keeping busy because it made the time fly. I had gone to the front to ask one of the receptionist for some paperwork on a potential customer, and I noticed that Marie was out front flirting with a guy who had come in to apply for a loan. Shari walked by and whispered in my ear, "Look at that nasty bitch. No wonder she got five kids and four baby daddies."

I chuckled and grabbed the paperwork I needed from the receptionist and headed back into my office. I was going over the applicant's file when my office phone rang. It was Jamaal.

"Good afternoon baby," he said sounding down.

"Good afternoon," I replied.

"How's your day going?" he asked.

"Not so bad," I answered. "And how's your day going?"

"It's going good. I mean we had a few problems with customers that want the work done but complain about the fees but that's nothing new. Aside from that things are running smooth though."

"That's good," I said showing no sign that I was still dwelling on our argument from the previous day. "So what are you making for dinner?"

"Steak and garlic mashed potatoes with green beans," I answered.

"Mmm, that sounds good. Well I was just calling to see how your day was going...so I'll see you when I get home."

"Alright," I said. "I love you Ni."

"I love you, too," I responded.

I picked up my paperwork and started reviewing it when Shari walked in my office and closed the door behind her. "You know that nosey ass receptionist told Marie what I said to you?

"She did?" I said.

"Yeah as soon as Marie walked back in from out front, she called her over and started whispering to her in Spanish."

"And how you know that she was telling her about that?" I asked. "Because the bitch looked over at me and rolled her eyes and then she walked away mumbling some shit in Spanish. That bitch knew better than to talk shit in English. She knows how close I am to beating her ass."

"Don't even trip over her, girl. If she wasn't bold enough to talk that shit she was talking in English then just leave it alone. Besides, you don't want her going and call Mr. Edwards because it always seems to fall back on your ass, and this time you just might really end up losing your job."

"Oh, if I lose my job I'm beating her ass, and I mean that, Ni'raisha."

"Just be easy," I said. There was a knock on the door. "Come in," I said.

"Hey is everything cool?" It was Jessica. She worked in the Customer Service Department and was one of the cool girls. Her and Shari were the only women in the office that I dealt with, but I still didn't trust either of them enough to share my business with them.

"Yeah. Why'd you ask that?" Shari said.

"Because I heard Marie talking shit in Spanish," Jessica said.

"What was she saying?" I asked.

"She said that Shari was a jealous bitch and that she can't wait until she's gone. She had said something to Tanya and she said 'watch,' like she was gonna do something."

"Watch what? She ain't gonna do shit," Shari said. That bitch is all talk."

Jessica laughed. "Don't know why she is like that. If you don't wanna be in her little crew then she gotta have some kind of drama with you."

"Yeah but she can't stand, Shari," I said. "That's because I don't put up with her shit like everybody else does. I'm my own person, and Marie don't run shit over here."

"You just gotta learn to ignore her ignorant ass and stop letting her get to you," I said.

Jessica shook her head in agreement.

"Ya'll better go ahead and get back to work before she calls Mr. Edwards and starts snitching," I said.

"I know. Come on, Shari," Jessica said. "I'll see you around Ni'raisha," she joked as she left my office.

I laughed to myself and thought, "This is one crazy ass place," as I resumed my responsibilities. I looked at the time on my desktop computer. "Just two hours and fifteen minutes to go," I mumbled. I just couldn't wait for the day and more so the week to be over.

When I got home, L.T. had already had his homework finished and was in his room playing his Playstation three. I loved the fact that he was so mature and responsible for his age. I had given him his own house key to get in the house when he got home from school because he didn't like the idea of having to always go to my mom's house afterschool. He had asked me to give him a chance to prove himself, and so I did, and he had not made me regret it yet. I'd never come home to a messy house or a house full of kids.

"Ma, what's for dinner?" he asked.

"Food," I joked as I seasoned the steak in a big bowl.

"Ooh, you making steak? That's what's up." He made his way into the den to finish playing his video game that he had paused.

I put the steak in the oven and walked over to the telephone to call Tay. The number was out of service so I took it that she stuck to her word about not wanting Ty to contact her. I would just have to wait for her to call me with her new number.

I walked into the living room and turned on the television when the phone rang. "Hello," I said.

"Hey girl."

"And how are we feeling today?" I asked.

"I'm alright," Tay answered. "Ty came back here last night and tried to use the key to get in, but I fooled his ass 'cause I changed the locks."

I laughed. "So what did he do?"

"He was banging on the door all crazy, and I told him to go back to that bitch."

"And he just left?"

"What else he is he gonna do, call the cops? His name ain't on this lease, and I'm keeping everything in this house. I threw all of his clothes out on the front stoop and he took them. His black ass just better be lucky that I'm trynna work on myself or I might have burned them."

"I hear that." I said. "So did you go job hunting today?"

"Yeah and nothing came up, but I faxed my resume over to this real estate company that's looking for a receptionist. They called me to set up an interview for Tuesday morning at eight thirty. It's not a guarantee but it's a start"

"That's great. And what are the hours?"

"Eight thirty to 4:30. It's a 40 hour a week position from Monday through Friday. I figured if I get it at least I'll have the weekends off."

"You really on your job, huh?" I asked.

"Ni, I know that you probably thought that I was playing and so did Natty, but this time I meant it. Things are only about to get better for me."

"I know," I said. "Tay?"

"What's good?"

"I gotta tell you something but you can't say anything to Natty because you know how she is."

"What happened?" Tay asked.

"You know that guy Ron that I met a couple of months ago when we were at the mall?"

"You mean the one you had went out with when you lied and told Jamaal you was with me?"

"Yes," I replied. "Oh God, Ni, what did you do?"

"Nothing too bad. I went to his house yesterday after Jamaal and I got into an argument. Jamaal got upset after Mark had approached him about whether or not he had told me about seeing him at the pool hall with that chick."

"Oh, Jamaal seen him with the bitch? I didn't know all of that."

"Yeah, and he told me and that's why I was so intent on catching his ass but I never told Natty about it and Jamaal seems to think I did. He told me I should have just minded my business."

"And if it was his boy he probably would have done the same thing," Tay added.

"Exactly, but I didn't tell Natty anything. She had already told me that she thought he was creeping and that's why I told her we were gonna follow him."

"Well regardless he shouldn't have come off at you like that. It ain't like Mark punk ass was gonna do shit anyways."

I laughed.

"But what happened when you got to Ron's house?" Tay asked.

"We was chillin watching a movie and he started kissing me. Then things started heated so I got up and left."

"So basically you kind of cheated on Jamaal."

"I wouldn't call it cheating. It was just a kiss."

"So what are you gonna do now? You gonna keep seeing him?"

"I don't know. I'm really starting to like him-"

Tay interrupted, "But is it worth losing Jamaal?"

"Of course it's not, Tay. But you know how it is once you start dealing with someone, it's kind of hard to end it. Especially if you find yourself really feeling that person. In a way, I wish I never called him and I hadn't even spoken to him in almost two months up until yesterday."

"Well you know that I am not gonna judge you, Ni, 'cause you my girl, and I got ya back just like you always have mine but just make sure that your willing to accept whatever comes out of this." Tay said.

I couldn't believe this. For once my best friend was really making sense. I always knew she had it in her. "I know. I just gotta figure out where I'm gonna go with all of this."

I heard keys jingling in the door and Jamaal walked in. "I'll call you back Tay." I said knowing that she would get the hint that he was home.

"Okay." Click.

I walked into the kitchen and pretended to be checking on dinner.

"It smells good," Jamaal said.

"Thanks," I replied.

Jamaal walked into the living room and sat on the couch. He took his boots and sat them on the shoe rack next to the door and then headed into the Den with L.T. I took a deep breath. I didn't know what I was going to do but one thing was for sure, I knew I had to make a decision and soon.

Chapter 7

Christmas was just right around the corner, and the snow had already began to fall. I hadn't spoken to Tay or Natty in a few days, and things were just getting back to normal with Jamaal and me. It was mid-morning Friday and I would be leaving work at noon to attend a conference at L.T's school. I notified my supervisor that I would be taken the rest of the day off. Any time away from that place was time well spent. The fact that I had started resenting my job was a sign that it was time to start searching for a new job and that was exactly what I planned to do right after the New Year.

When Saturday finally arrived, I was somewhat excited about seeing Ron. Jamaal, L.T., and I would first go bowling and then afterwards I would head out to meet up with Ron. After breakfast, Jamaal and L.T. headed to the Y for one of their usual basketball games. I picked up the phone and called Natty to see what she had been up to.

"Good morning," I said.

"Good morning, Ms. Thang she replied. "And what are you up to this morning?"

"Just relaxing until L.T. and Jamaal get back from their basketball game," I said. "Then I'm gonna fix them some lunch and later on we're going bowling."

"Oh, that sounds fun. The only time Mark and I did things like that was when we first got together, but after we had Tashaya all of that shit went right out the window. We hardly ever did things like that with the kids and when the kids did get the opportunity to go out and enjoy events, I was the only one there with them. Mark didn't even as much attempt to pick up a ball and take MJ to play basketball."

"That's because Mark didn't have his priorities straight," I said.

"His little girlfriend has no idea what she has gotten herself into," Natty said.

"I just don't understand what will make her think that he won't do the same thing that her that he did to you," I said.

"She probably don't even care as long as he keeps the money coming in," Natty said.

"Hmm. So I guess she doesn't mind selling herself short but she wouldn't be the first. Any female that deals with a man and sleeps with him just because he's got money and is supporting her needs, is no different from a prostitute or a call girl if you ask me."

"I couldn't agree more," Natty replied.

"Nowadays that's just how it is, though. People are in relationships for all of the wrong reasons. You got a few people who are really in love and don't care about the materialistic shit as long as they have the one they love by their side. Then you got the other ones who are just in it for the money. The females run around bragging about how they fucked this dude and he bought them such and such or how a nigga wanted to fuck but he wasn't getting shit if he ain't pay up. And the new generation of men have become more dependent on women."

Natty said, "Hell yeah. Remember when we was younger? Didn't no man want a female taking care of him because he was the man of the house and he would feel like less of a man. But now niggas is just saying fuck it. They doing that same shit females be doing. They be running around bragging to their boys about how they got this chick who pushing a nice ass whip and what she be doing for them." Natty laughed.

"You ain't never lie girl.

"And don't even get me started on that show "Snapped" when the women be killing their boyfriends and husbands for insurance money. And some of them be killing them just so they can run off with another man. I just can't seem grasp the concept of why the hell they would wanna kill the man to be with someone else rather than just telling them that they don't wanna be with them and they moving on. Do they feel like they ain't gonna be happy with the new man unless the old one is dead or something?"

"No, they just stupid as hell," I replied. "Those women be killing their men for nothing 'cause they end up getting caught and still don't get nothing but life behind bars."

"Well they say that money is the route to all evil and they damn sure was right about that," Natty said.

I agreed.

"I spoke to Tay the other day and she was talking like she really means business this time around."

"I think she does," I replied. At that moment I felt like telling Natty about Ron but I just wasn't sure what she would say. I didn't want to hear her rant on about how wrong it was and especially considering her situation so I figured maybe another day. Maybe sometime in the future when she was completely over her divorce phase I would let her in on the details.

"I have to go and get the kids ready to go to their grandmother's house," Natty said.

"Okay so just give me a call tomorrow. I was thinking maybe me, you and Tay can go out and do a little Christmas shopping tomorrow if ya'll not busy. L.T. doesn't have much on his list this year so I figured I'd grab the things on his list in one shot and get it over with. Also, I wanted to go to a couple of jewelry stores and check out some watches for Jamaal."

"That sounds good," Natty replied. "The kids are gonna be at my mom's so I might as well do some Christmas shopping while they're gone. So just call Tay and see if she wants to come along."

"Alright," I replied.

"And tell Jamaal and L.T. that I said hello."

"Alright, I'll talk to you tomorrow."

The time was 6:30. Jamaal, L.T. and I had been at the bowling alley doing the family thing when a text alert came through my phone. It was Ron texting me to make sure that we were still on for the night. I went into the bathroom and texted him back to let him know that I would be at his house at about nine o'clock and headed back out to the floor. I didn't want Jamaal to become suspicious so I turned my phone on vibrate in case he had decided to reply back to my text. He texted me back saying that he would be waiting for me. Although I had felt a little bad about what I was doing, I couldn't control how I was feeling, and this is the way things were going to be for now. After bowling, we had gone out for ice cream and were home by eight. Jamaal and L.T. went into the living room to watch a movie and I went upstairs to freshen up. On my way down the stairs, I pretended to be on my cellphone with Tay. "Hey Tay." I said loud enough for Jamaal to hear. "I'm on my way now, girl."

I walked up to Jamaal and kissed him. "I'll be back later. I'm going to Tay's for a little while."

"Where's Ty?" he asked as he leaned back in the recliner.

"They're not together anymore."

"For how long?" he asked.

"For good I believe."

"Don't she got a job she needs to tend to?"

"No, she quit her job a week ago when her and Ty separated," I said. I made my way into the kitchen to grab my car keys off of the counter and Jamaal followed. "So what are you going to Tay house for?"

"I'm only going over there for a couple of hours, Jamaal."

"You're not answering my question, Ni."

"I'm just going to chill for a few. We ain't going out or nothing."

"Yeah but you don't usually go to Tay's house on the regular. What happened to the days when ya'll use to get up a couple of weekends out of the month?"

"Nothing happened. Tay has just been going through with her situation with Ty, and I've been trying to be her support system. We're best friends, and that's what we do. We stick by each other through thick and thin."

"But you starting to act like you don't wanna be home no more," he said.

I laughed. "That's not true, baby. You know I love being home with you. I'll tell you what. Next weekend is all yours," I said not sure if this was true. "No clubs, no friends, just me and you."

"It better be," Jamaal said accepting my promise. "L.T. goes to your parent's house damn near every weekend. I don't mind you hanging with your girls, but you hardly save any time for me anymore. We both work hard throughout the week so by the time we get home we eat, shower, and go to bed. The only time we really do things together is when L.T. is with us."

"Okay baby," I said. "Next weekend is our weekend." I kissed him, grabbed my keys off the counter and headed out the door.

When I arrived at Ron's house, he greeted me with open arms and a kiss. "You wanna watch a movie?" he asked.

"Sure," I said. "'Five Heartbeats'? That's a classic."

"You got it," Ron said as he browsed through his DVD collection neatly organized on the stand. Ron grabbed a blanket from the room and sat next to me on the couch. As I pushed myself closer to him to cuddle, he wrapped his arms around me. During the movie Ron continuously kissed on my neck. I had to admit he was making me moist between my thighs but I tried to maintain my composure. Toward the end of the movie, Ron got up and walked out of the living room. I figured he was just using the bathroom until he called for me to come join him in his bedroom. As soon as I had walked in the room he grabbed me and threw me down on the bed. He stood over me and took off his shirt. His six-pack abs just turned me on all the more. He leaned over to me and started kissing me as he unbuttoned my pants. I didn't object this time. The way he had been caressing me had felt too good for me to stop him now. Once he had removed every article of clothing, he worked his way down with his mouth. I was in a different world. After I climaxed, he reached into his side drawer and pulled out a Magnum. He wasted no time inserting his penis into my dripping wet vagina. It was an amazing moment that I couldn't regret if I wanted to and there was no turning back now. We made love for about 40 minutes before Ron relieved himself. After all was said and done, I had to admit that it was well worth it. I thought I would have felt guilty afterward, but being intimate with Ron just made me wanna go another round.

Ron got up and headed into the bathroom. He called out for me to come and get into the shower with him. While in the shower he asked me if I was sure Jamaal was the person that I wanted to spend the rest of my life with.

"Of course," I said. "Why'd you ask that?"

"Because if that was the case then you wouldn't be here with me."

I looked over at him and smiled. "I'm sure."

He laughed at me and continued washing up. He did make a good point, but I really did wanna be with Jamaal. I tried to think of it as getting it out of my system before I married Jamaal although I knew it sounded ridiculous.

After showering and getting dressed, I headed home to get some much needed rest.

It was Sunday morning, and I called Tay to see if she would be rolling with Natty and me but only got her voicemail. I left a message for her to call me back and then I called Natty to confirm our ladies outing. After confirming with Natty, I headed into the kitchen to make breakfast. L.T. and Jamaal were already in the kitchen sitting down.

"Good morning guys," I said as I walked in.

"Good morning, ma," L.T. replied.

"Good morning," Jamaal said in a low tone of voice. I walked over to the refrigerator to grab the eggs, sausages, and waffles out and then I walked over to the stove to prepare the food, Jamaal walked up behind me and kissed me on the neck. "Did you enjoy your night?"

"Yes I did," I replied.

"That's good," he said kissing me again but this time on the cheek. He whispered in my ear. "You know we're long overdue, right?"

I smiled and nodded.

After we had finished breakfast, I went up to the bedroom to take out something to wear. My cell phone rang and it was Tay calling. "Hey Ni. I'm sorry I missed your call. I was in church and left my phone in the car."

I had to make sure I heard her correctly. "You were where?"

"Yep. That's right," she said. "I was in church. I had to ask god for forgiveness."

"What made you wanna go to church? I just spoke to you last week and you didn't say anything about church to me."

"God is good, Ni. I was so worried about not being able to find a job to pay the rent on my new place and he came through."

"Hold on. So you got a job, too?"

"Uh huh. You remember that job interview that I told you I had last week?"

"The receptionist job?"

"Yes. I had gone to the interview, and they emailed me later on that day and told me that they decided to go with someone who was more qualified for the position so I ended up going to three temp agencies and applying for temp work. I prayed on it for two days, Ni. Then one of them called me back and called me in for an interview. They offered me a temp to permanent position as a data entry clerk paying $11 an hour."

"Tay, that's great! Congratulations!"

"Thanks, Ni. I know it's not what I would like to be making but it will get me by and I finally feel like I'm going somewhere in life."

"I'm so happy for you Tay. When do you start your new job?"

"Monday morning.

"Well that's good," I said. "You got rid of Ty, you got a job, and now you're going to church. Just last week you were worried about being stuck in this new lease at your new place because Ty just left you stuck with the rent. I must say that I am really proud of you."

"Thanks, Ni. And thank you for always being there for me."

"You're welcome, Tay. And things are only gonna get better from here."

"So what's going on for the day?" she asked. "Well actually that's what I was calling you for. Natty and I were gonna go and do a little Christmas shopping and we wanted to see if you wanted to tag along."

"Yeah, sure. I'll come with ya'll. Just give me about a half-hour to shower and change clothes," Tay said.

"Alright, well I'm about to get dressed myself so just call Natty's phone when you're ready because we're taking her car so she is coming to pick me up."

"Okay. I'll see you soon."

I hung up the phone and made my way upstairs to get dressed.

Chapter 8

Christmas had come and gone and New Years was days away. Ron and I had begun spending more time together than usual. We had started going shopping together, out to eat locally, and I had even spent a night out with him at the Holiday Inn while telling Jamaal that Tay, Natty, and I were having a ladies night sleepover. It had now become more than a weekend thing with Ron and I and any chance I got to spend with him, I had to take advantage of. I had gotten so careless that Jamaal had started to assume that something was going on. A few times I had told him that I was with Tay when I was with Ron and Tay had called the house for me because I didn't answer my cell phone, so I would lie and tell him that I ended up with Natty instead. As much as I wanted to refrain from hurting Jamaal's feelings, I was too deep in with Ron. Although Tay had always had my back she didn't want to lie for me anymore and I respected that. No matter what I had to do, I always found a way to spend time with Ron. And my relationship with Ron had begun to tear my family apart. I was no longer spending as much time with Jamaal and L.T. had even started acting out in school over the past few weeks. I knew it wasn't right but I couldn't fight the feeling that I was now in love with two men.

The New Year was just a day away, and everything in my life had seem to be falling apart. I had been pulling in the parking lot of my job, and I saw three cop cars and an ambulance truck were in the lot. When I got upstairs Shari had been in handcuffs and that's when I knew that she must have kept good on her word. Employees from every department had made their way to our department and there was a lot of whispering taking place. Marie was in a corner with a police officer crying and ranting on as she made hand gestures toward Shari. The police officer was becoming very frustrated and warned her to calm down. From the look of things I could see why Shari had been the one getting arrested. Marie had a busted lip, a bloody nose, her hair was a hot mess, and she had blood all over her off white blouse. I asked Shari if she needed me to call anyone as she passed me. The officer stopped and turned Shari toward my direction, given her a moment to answer my question.

"Can you call my husband for me please?" she said.

"Sure," I said grabbing a sticky note from off of the receptionist's desk. I took down Shari's husband's name and number and the officer grabbed her arm signaling that it was time to go. I walked into my office and closed the door behind me. I picked up the phone and dialed her husband's number to fill him in on the details. After ending my call with Shari's husband, there was a knock on the door.

"Come in," I said.

Jessica came walking in. "Hey Niraisha," she said closing the door behind her."

"Are the police gone?" I asked her.

"Yeah, they just left," she answered.

"What happened?" I asked her.

"Marie was trying to be funny so she came up to Shari and demanded that she make some copies for her and she told her ass straight out, hell no. she told Marie that she is not her supervisor and she had her own work to do. So then Marie told her that she didn't care who her supervisor was. She said she was V.P and she was requesting that she get those copies made right away so that they can be mailed out. When Shari refused to do as she said, she called hers truly, Mr. Edwards. The next thing I knew, Mr. Edwards was on the phone with Shari telling her that he was letting her go and that he couldn't have an office full of females who didn't want be team players and help each other out. Shari came out of her office and just started swinging on Marie and boy did she beat that ass." Jessica laughed.

"So once again Marie got her way, huh?"

"Yep. And she did that shit on purpose. She knew what she doing by demanding that Shari make those copies for her. All of her little homegirls have been sitting their asses around all day so she could've easily asked them but I think she knew that she could get Shari all riled up. Shari doesn't even work for her department and that's more the reason why Mr. Edwards was dead wrong for letting her go."

I agreed. "And if he said that he didn't want the drama at the job then he should have let both of them go. How the hell does she always seem to get the say so in who goes?"

"Hmmm. You know Marie and Mr. Edwards got this real close relationship so he never goes against her. It's like he fires people every week and most of them are people that do their job but just have drama with Marie."

"Where is Marie now?" I asked.

"She went in the ambulance to the hospital with her dramatic ass."

"That's crazy," I said shaking my head.

"Well, I'm about to go make these deposits so I will see you when I get back," Jessica said.

"Okay," I replied.

When Jessica opened the door to exit my office I peeked out. Everyone pretty much had resumed their normal daily routine but I was sure that any free moment that they had to reminisce about the fight, they would take advantage of. Things were as quiet as they had been in what felt like months. It was first thing in the morning and my stomach was already growling. I picked up my phone and texted Ron to see if he wanted to grab a bite to eat at lunch time. Unfortunately, Ron said that he was going to be taking care of business over the next few days so he would holla at me when he was straight. The one thing that I disliked about Ron was that although we were seeing each other more on a regular basis, he would sometimes make plans with me and not be able to follow through. Something would always come up but I knew that was what came along with his lifestyle and I had already chosen to accept it. In the past three weeks he had stood me up at least four times but I wasn't too bothered by it because we did see each other more than we had previously. I guess I would have to wait until he took care of his business and then we would get together for pleasure.

I had just finish preparing a small meal for Jamaal and I when he walked in the kitchen and asked me if we were picking L.T. up from my mom's or if we were going to wait until the following day.

"We can pick him up tomorrow. Since it's New Years, I was thinking that maybe I can invite Tay and Natty and you can invite of few of your friends over to celebrate. I can go and grab some champagne."

"That sounds like a plan." Jamaal said. "I'm gonna go and call a few of the guys to see if they wanna come over." He walked into the living room.

I picked up my cell phone to call Tay and Natty. I was hoping that they wouldn't be too upset with me. For the past few weeks, we hadn't spoken much because I had been trying to balance out spending time with Ron as well as Jamaal and L.T.

"Hey stranger," Tay said. "You've been keeping really busy huh?"

Knowing that I had to be careful about what I said, I ignored the question. "How's church?" I asked.

"Couldn't be better," Tay answered. "And work is wonderful. It's nothing like your job."

"Aren't you lucky," I said. "Anyways, Jamaal and I are having a few friends over tonight to celebrate the New Year so I was calling to see if you wanted to come over."

"I'll come, but the only thing I will drink is wine so don't try and peer pressure me," Tay said.

I laughed. "You don't have to drink liquor. Jamaal and the guys are probably gonna have some beer and liquor, but I'm gonna grab some wine and champagne for us. There's no harm in drinking wine and you go to church so you should know."

"I already agreed to have some wine Ni. Now what time should I be at your house?"

"Well it's 6:30 now," I said looking at my watch. "So let's say about 9:30."

"Alright, I'll see you in a few," Tay said.

I pressed end on my phone and scrolled through my contact to find Natty's number. The phone rang and Natty picked up.

"Hello," she said.

"Hey Natty," I said.

"Oh hey Ni. And how are we this evening?"

"I'm good and yourself."

"I'm managing," she answered.

"Are the kids with you tonight?"

"No there at my mom's. They've been over there since the day after Christmas, but I'm going to go and pick them up tomorrow 'cause it's back to school in a few days."

"Yeah I know. We're going to get L.T. from my mom's tomorrow, too," I said. "But Jamaal and I are inviting a few friends over tonight to celebrate the New Year and I was wondering if you would like to join us?"

"Well I damn sure didn't have anything else to do so I guess you can count me in. I'm glad you called 'cause I was just gonna stay in bed in take a bottle of champagne to the face."

"Great," I said. "Well you just be your butt at my house at 9:30"

"Alright," Natty replied. "I'll see you soon." Click.

"Jamaal baby," I yelled into the living room. "I'll be back in about thirty minutes!"

"Where you going? You didn't even eat dinner yet," he said as he peeked into the kitchen.

"I'm running to the liquor store and the grocery store to grab some appetizers. I'll eat when I get back. Do you need anything?"

"No I'm good, baby. Thanks for asking."

I grabbed my Michael Kors bag and my keys and went on my way.

Friday had finally arrived and after work I would go and pick up L.T. from home to take him to my mom's house. Then I would be meeting up with Ron at the mall to do a little shopping and hang out for a bit.

Things had definitely calmed down in the office since the incident with Marie and Shari had taken place. I had to give it to Shari though because she had really calmed Marie down and although we all knew that she was still a gossiper, she had been careful about letting anyone outside of her little fan club over hear her talking about other employees. Marie had suffered a broken nose and a busted lip at the hands of Shari and it was hilarious to see her walking around trying to be nice to everyone. My guess was that she had never suffered an ass kicking like that before. "Well mama always did say that when you beat their ass they won't fuck with you no more," I thought to myself. I grabbed a few files off of the corner of my desk to start working on. As I finished reviewing the first application I could sense that today would be a bad day for this applicant.

"Hey baby," Ron said as he walked up to me in front of F.Y.E. We exchanged a passionate kiss and then we made our way through the mall. "You're a very busy person," I said jokingly. "Yeah, well you know I gotta get this money," he replied with a smile on his face. We walked into Champs to look at the sneakers. Ron must have had at least 50 pairs of Nikes lined up in Nike boxes in his walk in closet. He picked up a sneaker off the wall display. "These are tight. You like these?" he asked me. I took the sneaker out of his hand to try and get a better glance at it.

"Yeah. Those are hot," I said.

Ron looked over to one of the sales people. "Yo, you got these in a 10?" he asked. The sales person walked over toward us to get a closer look at the sneaker. He told Ron that he would go to the back to check and see if they had any in his size. While we waited for him to return we continued to browse the store. Ron had seen a pair of Nikes that he thought would look cute on me. "You like those?" he asked pointing up at the Nikes on the display.

"They alright," I replied.

"You want 'em?" he asked.

"No, I'm good." I said not knowing if it would increase Jamaal's suspicions. Ron had been buying me things constantly for a couple of months and I did not want Jamaal asking questions. The things that Ron bought me were things that I wouldn't normally buy. Some of the things Ron bought me were way out of my budget. He must have bought me at least three pair of sneakers and five pair of high-priced shoes including a pair of

Louboutin shoes priced at $500. I would keep them in my car to hide them from Jamaal. The only time I had worn a few of them was when Ron and I went out together and I would change back into the shoes that I had on before I entered the house. For Christmas he had bought me a fourteen-karat tennis bracelet that I was barely able to wear unless I was with him. I kept that inside of the arm rest of my car. I didn't want any material things from Ron. All I had wanted was him, but I guess this is something that he was accustomed to when dealing with females.

The salesperson walked up to us with the size ten Nike box and handed it to Ron.

"Yo. Let me get those in a six," he said pointing to the pink and black Nikes that he had just asked me if I had wanted. "And let me get these in a ten, too, if you got em," he said as he took a pair of wheat Timberlands off of the display shelf."

"Okay," the salesman said nodding. "I'll be right back."

"You know you really don't have to do this Ron," I said.

"But I want to," he replied. "Now stop complaining and just accept it aight?"

"Alright," I said.

The salesperson came walking out of the back with two boxes in his hand. He opened them up so that we can check them out. "Are you guys all set?" he asked handing the boxes over to Ron.

"Yeah, we good," Ron replied.

"Okay. I can ring you up," he said walking toward the cash register.

Ron paid for the merchandise, and we headed to the food court to grab a bite to eat. We ordered a sandwich from Subway and then sat down to eat.

"So how was your day at work?" Ron asked.

"Not bad," I answered. "A couple of the girls had gotten into a fight on Monday and one of them had gotten arrested."

"Word," Ron laughed. "What happened?"

"One of the girls had kept intentionally messing with one of the other girls and got her fired so she beat dat ass." I laughed.

"Damn. It's just a whole bunch of entertainment up in there, huh?" he asked.

"Hell yeah," I replied. All that's missing is the camera crew. We get some of those and we can make some money up in that joint."

Ron laughed. "You know that can be arranged."

The next thing I knew, I heard someone calling my name. I looked back to see that it was Natty and she was heading my way. "Oh shit," I mumbled.

"Hey Ni," she said looking confused.

"Hey Natty. What are you doing here?" I asked.

"Just doing a little shopping," she said as she took a quick glance at Ron and then turned her head back to me. It got quiet for a few seconds and then I broke the silence.

"Oh Natty, this is Ron." I said.

"Hi," Natty said in a rude tone of voice. "Where's L.T.?"

"At my mom's," I answered.

"Oh. Alright then. I'll talk to you later," she said.

"I'll call you," I said as Natty walked away. I knew that this couldn't be good because I would be stuck hearing her mouth the next time that we spoke.

We finished eating and conversing and then we headed back to Ron's for dessert. We entered the house and removed our shoes. We went into the bedroom to watch some television. I had been a little nervous about Natty now knowing about my affair with Ron. If she had seen us together then it was possible that someone else might had as well. I shook the thought off. We were laying down watching TV when Ron reached over and into his side dresser drawer. He pulled out a small piece of aluminum foil that had been balled up. Ron had opened up the foil and there was a white substance inside.

"What is that?" I asked.

"Don't worry about it," he replied.

Although I asked the question I wasn't stupid and had known that it was cocaine. I knew he had smoked weed, but I had no idea that he did coke. Ron picked up his phone and turned it off as he would usually do when we were trying to spend some quality time which was a plus for me. When we had first started spending time together his phone was ringing off the hook to the point where it was starting to annoy me so as a favor to me he had stop taking calls on our time.

"Come here," he said.

"For what?" I asked.

"Just come here," he said taking a dollar twenty dollar bill from his pocket. I crawled over to his side of the bed. "Take this," Ron said as he handed me the bill. He grabbed a playing card from the deck of cards on his dresser and made two line on his nightstand with the coke. "Pass me that," he said taking the bill from my hand. He started rolling the bill tightly and then he sniffed some of the coke up through it.

I looked at him in surprise.

"Here try it," he said rubbing his nose.

"No. I don't do that shit," I said shaking my head.

"Ain't nothing gonna happen to you. It's just gonna make you feel numb but good. You smoke weed before, right?"

"Yeah when I was like eighteen."

"Well, you know the feeling you get when you smoke weed? That's how it's gonna make you feel."

"If that's the case then why ain't everybody who smoke weed sniffing then huh? 'Cause that's not true."

"Yo just try it this one time and I promise I will never ask you again," he said.

After a few minutes of Ron begging me, I decided that I would just try it out this one to me to shut him up and that would be it. He passed me the bill and instructed me to hold one nostril closed with my finger. I sniffed up the other line that he had on the nightstand. I couldn't believe what I was doing. I started feeling weird. I was feeling numb and light-headed and when I glanced over at Ron, he seemed just fine. He had started fiddling with his nose as if it was itching, and his eyes were big and red. I could only imagine how I had looked but then again he had emptied the foil. He climbed on top of me, and we made love until we were both satisfied. He rolled over and went to sleep and I climbed out of the bed and got dressed. I was still feeling woozy, so I went into the bathroom and threw some cold water on my face. I was a little fidgety and I had to get it together before I got home. I went into Ron's refrigerator and grabbed a cold bottle of spring water.

I locked the bottom lock of Ron's door and then headed home. When I got in the house Jamaal was not there. He had told me that he didn't have any plans on going anywhere but I figured that maybe he ended up going out with some friends. I picked up the phone and called Natty to explain the situation to her but her phone had gone to voicemail. I was still feeling a little dazed so I turned down the heat and took a cool shower. Once I had gotten out of the shower I called Jamaal's phone to see what time he would be coming home but I didn't get an answer so I left him a message letting him know that I was at home waiting for him. I turned off the light and laid in my bed in the dark until I fell asleep

Sunday morning had arrived and I had awaken with the thoughts of what had taken place the night before. I went downstairs, and Jamaal was already dressed in the living room watching TV.

"You want some breakfast?" I asked as I headed into the kitchen.

"Nah, I'm good."

"I'm gonna stop by Dunkin Donuts and grab something after I pick up L.T."

"Okay," I said as I walked over to the cabinet and took out the can of Folgers coffee. Jamaal came walking into the kitchen. "So what time did you get in last night?" I asked him.

"I don't know. Maybe 1:30, 2 o'clock. Why?"

"Why didn't you answer your phone when I called?"

"Because I didn't hear it ringing," Jamaal replied. Jamaal's phone rang and he grabbed his black fatigue coat that was hanging on one of the kitchen chairs. He came over and kissed me. "I'll be back in a few," he said as he headed out.

I made a cup of coffee and then went into the living room to watch television. As I flipped through the channels, when I couldn't find anything to grab my attention, I picked up the phone to call Tay.

She answered the phone. "Hello."

"What's up Tay?" I asked.

"Hey Ni. I was just on my way out the door for church."

"Oh okay." I said. I had been so proud of Tay for the changes that she was making in her life and for a brief moment I actually had regret about my affair with Ron. "I saw Natty yesterday," I said.

"Where did you see her at?"

"She was at the mall and I had been sitting down eating with Ron when she approached us."

"Really? So what did she say?" Tay asked.

"Nothing much. She was just looking all funny in the face but she kept it cool. She didn't try to blow up my spot or nothing but I could tell that she was definitely not feeling it."

"Wow. That's crazy," Tay said. "Well we gotta go and pick up our dresses from the tailor next weekend so get ready to hear it."

"I know."

"Let me get going so that I won't be late for church. I'll call you when I get back."

"Alright," I replied. Click.

I picked up the phone to call Natty again but once again I got the voicemail. This time I left a message. "Hey Natty, it's Ni. Give me a call when you get this message okay?" I hung up the phone.

Chapter 9

February had finally arrived, and things had really gotten out of hand with Ron and myself. On the other hand, Tay was doing well. She was still working and going to church trying to become a better individual. Natty and I had hardly spoken anymore. The last time we had seen each other was when we went and picked our dresses. She had asked me why I was still seeing him and once I assured her that I was going to let my affair with Ron go, she hadn't spoken of it since. I think that giving the situation she had gone through with Mark, she was very disappointed to find out that I had been cheating on Jamaal. Jamaal and I had become more distant, and L.T.'s grades had been slipping in school. I was now at a place in my life where I never wanted to be, and I became so paranoid that I started to feel as if people were starting to suspect that I was on drugs. I was lost and confused and no longer in my right state of mind. I just wanted everything to be good again but I couldn't let Ron go.

I was at work sitting at my desk and I hadn't been feeling well. I thought that maybe the drugs were really taking a toll on me. I had been feeling this way for the past couple of weeks but wasn't sure of what I should do. I couldn't just go to my doctor and tell her that I was possibly not feeling too well because I had been on drugs. I jumped up out of my seat and grabbed the garbage can. After vomiting for about a few minutes, I tied the small bag up and headed to the bathroom to clean myself up. "

Are you alright?" the receptionist asked as I walked past her desk.

"Yeah, I'm fine. Thanks for asking," I replied. I went into the bathroom and started rinsing my mouth out. I looked in the mirror at myself and I really didn't look too well. I would have to call my doctor and make an appointment but at no point would I blame the reason for my sickness on drugs. I picked up the small trash bad and took it outside to the dumpster. When I got back upstairs, I called and scheduled a doctor's appointment for the following week. Then I locked my office door and laid my head down on my desk for a short nap. I just hoped that I wouldn't be feeling like this on the weekend because I would be spending Saturday with Ron.

My office phone rang and I lifted my head off of my desk to answer. "Good morning, this is Ni'raisha speaking. How may I help you?"

L.T.'s school was calling. They needed me to come to the school right away. L.T. had gotten into some trouble at school with another student. He had punched the kid in the face and threatened to kill him. When I hung up the phone with the principal, I grabbed my things off of my desk and headed over to my supervisor's office. I knocked on the door.

"C'mon in," she said. "Mrs. Wright."

"Yes," she answered looking up at me.

"I have to take the rest of the day off. I had just gotten a call from my son's school and they need me to come down there," I said not wanting to get into specific details.

"Is he okay?" she asked. "Yeah, he's fine. Something had just taking place with him and another student and they need me to come down there for an emergency meeting." She looked at me with disappointing look on her face and exhaled, "Ok but just be aware that you have been missing a lot of work lately and I'm gonna have to write you up with a warning."

"Okay," I said not caring at the moment. I turned around and walked out closing the door behind me. I wasn't upset with Mrs. Wright because she had been telling the truth about me missing a lot of work lately and if I wasn't missing work then I was leaving early just to try and squeeze in some free time for Ron. When I got into the car I dug into my purse to get my phone out to call Jamaal.

"Hey Ni," he said as if he didn't really want to be bothered.

"Hey baby," I said. I'm on the way to L.T.'s school.

"Why, what happened?" he asked. "The principal just called me and told me that L.T.

had punched another kid in the face and threatened to kill him."

"What! Why'd he do that?" Jamaal asked.

"I don't know, but I will find out when I get there."

"Do you need me to leave work and meet you there," he asked.

"No, it's alright. You can handle him when you get home. When I leave his school, I'm gonna drop him off to my mom's and go back to work," I lied.

"Well make sure you let him know that I'm gonna have a talk with him when I get home." "Alright," I said.

"Oh and I'm running a little behind on work today so I'll be home late." Jamaal said. "Okay," I said. "I'll see you when you get home."

"Alright," I said. Click.

In all of these years Jamaal and I had been together he had never worked late this much. He had been working late for the past month and I was starting to suspect that he was cheating.

I picked up the phone and called Ron. "What's up, baby?" Ron said as he answered the phone.

"Hey, what are you doing?"

"I'm on the block. Why?" What's up?"

"Well I was going to my son's school for a meeting and then I was gonna come and see you."

"Oh you trynna get a quickie, huh?"

I laughed. "I got enough time for the real thing."

"Aight well call me when you on your way to my crib and I'll meet you there."

"Alright," I said. "I'll see you in a few."

As I entered the school and made my way into the office I could see L.T. through the glass. He had an angry look on his face.

The principal walked up and greeted me. "Hi, Ms. Rakes. How are you?"

"I'm fine and yourself?"

"I'm good. Thanks for asking," she said. "Can you step into my office?" She motioned for L.T. to follow. "Have a seat," she said pointing to two empty chairs. She started explaining to me that L.T. had attacked another child and threatened him as well.

When I asked L.T. for an explanation, all he could say was that the other student made him angry.

"Well Leonard," I said addressing him by his government name. "You don't just go around hitting or threatening people because they make you angry. The fact that he made you mad doesn't make what you did right."

L.T. sat in the chair with his mouth poked out.

"What exactly did this other student say to you to upset you?" I asked.

"He kept picking on me saying that's why my dad was in jail and I'll never be able to see him again."

"Well how did he know that your dad was in jail?" I asked.

"Because I told him when we were friends and ever since the new kid came in our class, he's been acting brand new toward me."

L.T.'s principal interrupted. "Regardless of what the cause was, Leonard, that does not justify you attacking another student. It's against our school policy .and we cannot have this type of violence occurring at our school."

I agreed. "Leonard, you cannot let stuff like that get to you. Throughout your life you are going to meet a lot of people that have bad things to say about you or your family. All that matters is that you love your family and we love you back."

"I actually have a meeting with the other student's parents this afternoon, and I will be sure to advise them of their child's actions as well," the principal said.

I nodded.

"Mrs. Rakes, can I talk to you alone for a minute?" she asked.

"Sure," I replied. I asked Jamaal to wait outside of the office for me.

"I wasn't aware that Leonard's dad was incarcerated," she said.

"Yes, he is and he has been incarcerated since Leonard was five."

"Well is there anyone else that is in his life at this time?"

"Yes, my fiancé but honestly I don't understand how this pertains to the situation."

"I apologize if you think that I am getting into your personal life, but it's just that a lot of children tend to act out when one parent is not active in the child's life."

"Well he has a stepfather who is very involved in his life," I said.

"Is there anything going on at home that would trigger him to act out? Up until a couple of months ago Leonard's behavior was up to par, so I'm just trying to piece together what the problem might be."

"I don't mean to be rude, but are you a psychologist?"

"No I am not," she answered. "But I have been in my field of work for eleven years now, and I can't tell you how much I see situations like this one occur. And majority of the time it has something to do with changes that have taken place inside of the home."

"Well everything inside of our household is just fine but thank you for being concerned."

"Okay," she said as she stood up from the chair at her desk. "Well right now Leonard is just being suspended for three days for his actions, but you do realize that he could have very well been arrested or even expelled for threatening that other child?"

"Yes, I am aware of that and when we get home his step dad and I will sit down and have a talk with him," I replied.

"Alright," she said handing me a piece of paper from off the top of her desk. "Here are the terms of his suspension and it has been a pleasure talking with you." She shook my hand.

"Same here," I said taking the paper from her hand. I walked out of the office and signaled for L.T. to follow.

While in the car, I once again asked L.T. what the cause was for his behavior.

"I don't know," he said.

"What do you mean you don't know? There's a reason why you're all of a sudden acting up in school, and it has nothing to do with someone saying something about your dad. How many times have someone said something to you that you didn't like and you ignored it? So you're telling me that of all the things that have been said this is the only one you couldn't ignore?"

L.T. shrugged.

"Answer the question!" I yelled.

Tears started rolling down L.T.'s eyes. "I'm just mad," he said.

"Mad about what?" I asked him.

"You and dad are not close like you use to be. First you were never home and now daddy. I'm at grandma's house all of the time now, and we don't even go out and do things together anymore the way that we use to. I already lost one dad, and now I feel like I'm about to lose another one." L.T. wiped tears with his coat sleeve.

I pulled the car over and looked over at L.T. "L.T., Jamaal's not going anywhere. He loves us and he's not just going to run off and leave us."

"Well then why are you two acting like you don't wanna be together anymore?"

"That's not true L.T. Jamaal and I are still very much in love. That's why we're getting married in four months," I said with a smile on my face. "Now give me a hug."

L.T. smiled and hugged me.

"Are you hungry baby?" I asked.

"Starving," L.T. said rubbing his stomach.

We're gonna go eat a McDonald's and then I'm gonna drop you off to grandma's because I have to go back to work."

"Okay," L.T. agreed.

Hearing L.T. talk like that really hurt me and the one thing that I didn't want was to see my baby hurting like this. While Jamaal and I had been going through our problems we forgot all about L.T. I decided that I needed to talk to Jamaal and plan a night out on the weekend for the three of us.

Ron's house was the usual same shit, different day. It had become a routine to go to his house, watch TV, do some blow, and have sex. Then I would head home afterwards. When I left Ron's house I headed to my mom's house to pick up L.T. and then we headed home. I took the chicken that I had already seasoned before I left for work and put it in the oven.

The house phone rang. "Hello," I answered.

"Hey Ni." It was Natty.

"Hey girl. What's been going on with you?"

"Oh not too much just working and taking care of these kids," she responded. "And what about you? You still running around having an affair?"

"You know you've been a really judgmental person lately."

"And does that make me a bad person because as a friend I would like to see you do the right thing and get your relationship back on track. You see what I went through and it wasn't a good feeling so how do you think Jamaal's gonna feel when he finds out?"

"Alright, Natty, but when you was going through your shit with Mark I was there for you. I didn't keep reminding you of how stupid you were for letting him control you, did I?"

"I'm not saying that you're stupid, Ni. I'm just saying that your about to ruin your marriage before it even starts."

"Well thanks for making me aware of that. I have to go and finish dinner now before Jamaal gets home. And don't forget we have to pick up the wedding favors next weekend."

"Alright, she said. "Give me a call tomorrow."

"Yep." I replied. I hung up the phone. Who in the hell did she think she was trying to tell me how to live my life? If she had been handling her business and shown some sign of independence, maybe Mark wouldn't have left her ass for someone with a job. She had just made me so angry and at the moment I wish that I had been with Ron. He would have made things so much better. My high had worn off and that was the one thing that I needed to get into my own zone and not let bullshit get to me. I felt good in high mode.

Jamaal came in the house and went upstairs. I followed him. "Are you going to eat dinner?" I asked.

"Nah. I'm not hungry. Where's L.T. at?" He asked as he sat down on the bed and removed his shoes.

"He's in his room lying down." I explained to him everything that took place at school and what L.T. had expressed to me in the car. I told Jamaal that I had promised L.T. that we would go out somewhere as a family in the weekend, and he agreed.

He stood up from the bed. "I'm about to go and talk to him and see what's going on."

As soon as Jamaal walked out of the room, I grabbed his wallet from the nightstand on his side of the bed and began looking through it. Jamaal coming home at seven in the evening and he was not hungry...something wasn't adding up to me. He had a credit card receipt in his wallet from the American Steakhouse. I checked the date and noticed that he had been out to eat. I knew that he hadn't eaten by himself because two meals had been printed out on the receipt as well as a bottle of wine. I closed his wallet back up and waited for him to come back into the room.

As soon as he came in the room, I closed the door behind him and started to question him. "Are you cheating on me Jamaal?"

He looked at me as if I were talking crazy. "No. What are you talking about? There is nobody else. I told you earlier that I had to work late today."

"So were you working late at the Steakhouse, Jamaal?" I said flashing the receipt in his face.

He looked down at it. After he realized that he had been caught, he walked over to his side of the bed and started undressing.

"So what, you ain't got nothing to say now?"

"Why does it matter, Ni? You think I don't know about that nigga you be running around here with?"

I got quiet.

Jamaal smirked. "Yeah. You don't have much to say now, huh?"

I knew that he had his suspicions but it was obvious that he had known more than I thought.

"You didn't think I knew?" he said standing up from the bed. "You wanna have your cake and eat it, too." Jamaal walked out of the room and into the bathroom to shower.

I was hurt and I couldn't believe Jamaal would do this to me, but then again who was I to talk? I had been unfaithful as well and would now get to experience Jamaal's pain..

I went downstairs to call Tay. She could sense the hurt in my voice. "What's wrong Ni?"

"Jamaal is seeing someone else," I said as tear drops came rolling down my face.

"How do you know that?" Tay asked.

"Because I found a receipt for two from the steakhouse, so I asked him about it and he basically admitted it."

"Ni, now you know you my girl and I love you, right?"

"Yeah," I replied.

"But you know what they say, what goes around, comes around."

I felt so stupid and was at a loss for words.

"Now it's up to the two of you to decide where ya'll are gonna go from here. It's either ya'll are gonna be together or not but whatever you and Jamaal decide to do just be sure to keep L.T. in mind. You don't want him being in the middle of all of this drama ya'll got going on."

I knew everything that Tay was saying made sense. "I know," I agreed. "I'm gonna call you tomorrow, girl 'cause I need to get some rest for work."

"Alright," Tay said. "And Ni?"

"Yes?" I replied as I wiped my face.

"I know what you're doing, and I'm not gonna judge you, but you know how the streets is always talking. I'm not about to sit here and preach to you, but as your best friend I'm begging you to get help before you not only hurt yourself but L.T. as well."

I didn't really want to respond to her statement. I just wondered how many other people knew about this.

"Maybe you should come with me to church one Sunday. It'll be fun and if you enjoy it maybe we can get L.T. and Jamaal to come along with you one day."

"We'll see what happens," I responded.

"Just let me know when you're ready," she said.

"Alright Tay, I'll call you tomorrow." Click.

I walked upstairs to the bedroom, and Jamaal was lying on his side in the bed. I looked at him wanting to apologize for my actions, but the thought of him seeing someone else kept me from saying something. I turned over on my side with my back toward his and cried myself to sleep.

When Saturday had finally arrived, we kept our word on taking L.T. out to eat. Everything was pretty quiet at the table, and Jamaal and I had barely said two words to each other since the night that I had found out he had been seeing someone else. I didn't want to make it any more obvious to L.T. than it already had been that our relationship was falling apart, so I struck up a conversation.

"So how was your week at work honey?" I said to Jamaal.

From the way Jamaal looked at me, I could tell that he really did not want to respond to my question.

"It was okay. It's been a very busy week," he said looking down at his plate.

"I bet it was. I could only imagine," I said with a smile on my face.

Jamaal ignored me and turned to L.T. "So what are we gonna do tomorrow?"

"I don't know; maybe go to the Y and shoot some hoops," L.T. replied.

"That sounds good," Jamaal said.

"And mom can come and watch," L.T. said.

"That's a good idea," Jamaal said.

"I'm pretty sure mommy has nothing to do tomorrow," he said with a smirk on his face.

L.T. looked over at me. "So Mom, are you gonna come?"

"Of course I am," I said.

"Yes!" Jamaal said giving L.T. a high five. "Mommy's finally gonna hang out with us again."

I knew that Jamaal was just being sarcastic, but I'd let him have this one. I wanted to see

Ron this weekend, but it was cool. I knew what L.T. was trying to do, and I was going to do whatever it took to make him happy.

Chapter 10

My doctor's appointment on Wednesday afternoon gave me an excuse to leave work early. On my way out, my supervisor passed me a white envelope that had been sealed. When I got into my car, I opened the envelope and took out the letter. It was another warning notice. Without reading it, I threw it in the glove compartment and drove off. I had really wished I would have stuck to my plan to find a new job after the New Year had come.

When I arrived at the doctor's office, I signed in and had a seat. About 15 minutes later, one of the nurses had called me in. she checked my vital signs and then asked me what all of my symptoms had been. She jotted the information down and then left out of the room. A few minutes later, Dr. Winn had come in and gone over what the nurse had written down. She wanted to run some test on me just to rule out anything serious but first she wanted me to do a urine test to rule out pregnancy. A few moments after I had taken a urine test, she came back into the room to let me know that pregnancy was indeed the reason why I had been feeling sick and vomiting a lot. She asked me when my last menstruation was and as much as I had wished I could remember, I couldn't recall. After having me lie down while she gently pressed down on my pelvis and my stomach,

Dr. Winn said that from what she could tell I was about eight weeks along but of course the ultrasound would be the only way to confirm this and my exact due date. She asked me if I knew what I was going to do or did I need time to think about it. I advised her that there was no doubt in my mind. I was keeping my baby for sure. One thing that I was against was abortion, and no child that I was carrying would become a statistic. After advising me that she was setting me up an appointment for an ultrasound to find out a due date, Dr. Winn once again congratulated me and wrote me out a prescription for prenatal vitamins. She said that we would schedule blood work for my next visit with her. I thanked Dr. Winn and headed out of the office in disarray.

Jamaal and I had been trying for years to have a baby, and now I wasn't even sure of whom the father was of this child that was growing inside of me. I didn't know how I was going to explain to Jamaal that I was pregnant and that it is possible that he is not the father. I was so confused because this is a moment that I should've have been excited about but I knew that nothing good could come from this. I would have to tell Jamaal because sooner or later it would come out considering there was no way I can hide my belly from him the whole pregnancy. This was no longer about me and the man that I had been having an affair with.

This was about the baby and it was only fair that I let both of them know the truth.

When I got into my car, I immediately called Tay. "Tay, I'm pregnant," I said.

"What! By who?" she asked.

"I don't know. I don't know what to do!" I yelled as I leaned my forehead against the steering wheel and broke down crying.

"Calm down and listen to me," she said. "You can't be stressing yourself out girl your pregnant. And it's not like stressing out and losing your head is going to change things. It's only going to make things worse."

I continued sobbing into the phone. "Where are you now?" she asked.

"I just left the doctor's office," I replied.

"Stop by my house," Tay said.

"Alright," I said reaching over into the glove compartment for a napkin. "I'll be there shortly." I pressed the end button and made my way over to Tay's house. on my way to Tay's all I could think about was how can this happen to me? This was not my life story, or at least I never imagined it would be. I was starting to feel hopeless.

"Hey girl," Tay said as she hugged me.

"Hey," I replied hugging her back.

"Come on in the living room and have a seat," she said.

I followed Tay into the living room. I looked around. "I like this Tay. You hooked this place up."

"Yeah, well don't get used to it cause I'm moving in three weeks," she said.

"Oh you are?"

"Yeah. I told you that once I found a job I was moving. Ty don't come by no more, but I wanna be sure that he doesn't even know where I live. I don't want to have any parts of him and his other relationship."

"Well, that's good," I replied.

"Okay now back to you girl. What are you going to do as far as this baby? You're keeping it right?"

"Of course. It's just that I don't know what to say to Jamaal or Ron."

"Tell them the truth, Ni. It wouldn't be right to lie to either of them regardless of who comes out to be the father of that baby, that baby is going to need its father," she said.

"I know," I replied.

"But honestly I can't see how it's gonna work out with Jamaal and I if he's running around having an affair himself."

"Did he say who the other woman was?" Tay asked.

"No. He was never even direct with me about cheating. All he said was that it didn't matter because I was running around with Ron."

"Well this is serious, and ya'll need to figure out whether the two of you are going to be together and make it work, or leave it alone. This is a child we're taking about. Can you do me a favor and come with me to church on Sunday?"

I looked at her with an unsure facial expression but I knew that I could use some prayer in my life at the moment. "Alright," I said.

"So we're on for Sunday right?" she asked.

"Yes. We're on. I promise," I said with a smile on my face.

Tay smiled back. "What's up with Natty? She just all of a sudden acts like she's too busy to be bothered. She was calling me damn near every day at one point."

"Maybe she got a man," I joked.

Tay and I talked a little more about my situation and her past situation, and it just felt weird that this time around she had been the one inspiring me.

"Well let me get home and prepare myself to break the news to Jamaal," I said to Tay as I took a deep breath. I'll probably see Ron tomorrow since it's Valentines' Day, but if not I will tell him over the weekend."

"Now see, Ni, that's what I'm talking about. Yeah you might be sleeping with Ron, but you are engaged to Jamaal. Why the hell are you over here making plans to spend such a special day with another man? You should be trying to plan something special for you and Jamaal and take the necessary steps to make your relationship right. I'm not gonna get in to your other situation and you know what I'm referring to, but now that you are pregnant I'm hoping that this will be your motivation to stop."

I knew that Tay was referring to my drug habit. I really didn't want to get into it so I changed the subject. "Oh, I forgot to tell you L.T. got suspended for fighting in school," I said.

"What? What happened? Tay asked.

"He said some boy in his class kept picking on him and talking about his dad."

"Oh my god. Well Ni, all you can do is pray on it," she said shaking her head. "And who is watching him?"

"Jamaal took the day off to keep an eye on him and tomorrow he is going to my mom's."

"He's a good man," Tay said. "Just make sure that you tell them both and make sure your real with Jamaal about you and Ron's relationship. Maybe he'll find forgiveness in his heart," Tay said.

"Okay. I will call you and let you know what happens."

As I pulled into the driveway, my stomach had started to turn. I was feeling so sick, and this time it wasn't from the baby. I walked into the house and Jamaal was in the living room watching television. "Hey," I said. "Where's L.T.?"

"Upstairs in his room," he answered without looking up at me.

"Did you guys make it to the mall?" I asked.

"Yeah. I got us a pair of sneakers."

"Oh, well that was nice," I replied. "Jamaal, I have to tell you something."

"What's up?" he asked.

"I'm pregnant."

Jamaal looked up at me. "By who?"

"What do you mean by that?"

"Look Ni," Jamaal said standing up. "I'm just asking because it's no secret that you been creeping with that thug ass drug dealing nigga. Pretty much everybody in Bridgeport and Stratford knows."

I looked at him with a terrified look. "I'm not sure," I said.

Jamaal shook his head. "Isn't it crazy when a female gets pregnant and don't even know who her baby daddy is?"

"It's not like I wanted things to be this way, Jamaal."

"If you didn't want things to be this way then they wouldn't!" Jamaal yelled. "Now I have to sit around and wonder whether my fiancé is pregnant by me or another nigga! What are we supposed to tell L.T., huh Ni? That mommy was running around sleeping with another guy so now we're not sure if she's pregnant by daddy or this other guy! The fucking wedding is off!" he yelled with tears forming in his eyes. He grabbed his keys off of the side table next to the couch and stormed out slamming the door behind him.

I sat down and put my face in my lap. I didn't know what to do. I loved him, and once I had seen how revealing my secret really hurt him, I had wished that I can take it all back. It was the day before Valentines' day and I would be spending it in hell. I needed someone else to talk to so I called Natty in hopes that she would answer.

"Hello," Natty answered.

"Hey Natty," I said. "Are you busy?"

"Not at the moment. What's up?"

"So I went to the doctor's today because I had been feeling sick lately only to find out that I'm pregnant."

"What!"

"I'm pregnant."

"Now are you pregnant with Jamaal's child or the guy I seen you at the mall with?"

"I don't know Natty. I just told Jamaal and he didn't take it well," I said.

"Well what did you expect, Ni? You had an affair behind your fiancés back and now you're not even sure who the father is."

"Why are you always so cold and judgmental when it comes to anyone other than yourself?"

"I'm just being real with you, Ni. That's what you want right? You don't want me to sit up here and act like you did nothing wrong 'cause then I would be being fake."

"Alright, alright. I'll talk to you later," I said hanging up without even waiting for a reply. I called Tay.

She answered the phone. "How's it going Ni?"

"I told Jamaal, and he just stormed out of the house pissed off," I replied.

"Well did he even respond when you broke the news to him?"

"Yeah but he was more distraught than anything. He said it's crazy because his fiancé is pregnant and doesn't even know if he is the father or the other nigga. Then I tried to call Natty just because I needed a friend to talk to and she just did a 360 on me. She blamed me for everything instead of backing me up. You know that I've always had Natty's back, Tay, no matter what."

"Yeah I know," Tay said.

"When she was going through her situation with Mark I was there. I even took time out of my day to go with her to see a damn lawyer."

"What is up with her?" Tay asked.

"I don't know but she's just been brand new lately huh? I understand that she might be upset with me for decisions that I've made because she has been cheated on but I have to learn from my own mistakes. It's not Natty or no one else's place except Jamaal to be upset at me for what I've done."

"And that is why I stress to you about, honesty Ni. I know that this is your life and you're going to make your own decision. All that I can offer you is feedback but rest assure that I will never turn my back on you because of the issues that you are having at this moment in your life because you were not always at this point. Everyone falls down, it's up to them whether they are going to stay down or get back up."

Tay was really a true friend and I really appreciated her words of wisdom. "I hung up on Natty and she didn't have to worry about me calling her anymore. When she learns to stop judging me then she can give me a call."

"Maybe she does have a new man and he got her acting up," Tay said.

"Or maybe that new car she just bought got her head gassed up." I added.

"She deserved to get the dial tone for that," Tay said.

About thirty minutes into our conversation Jamaal came walking in the door still visibly upset. "

I'll call you back Tay," I said.

Jamaal sat at the kitchen table and I walked up to him. "Are you okay?" I asked.

"Would you be okay if the shoe was on the other foot?" he asked.

"Of course not Jamaal, but I wanna try and work this out."

"How are we gonna work this out, huh? You're pregnant, and it's a big possibility that the baby is not even mine!"

"I know, Jamaal, and I'm sorry! I wanna end this all! I just want my family back!" I said as I started to cry. "I don't know who the father of this baby is but I'm praying that you are!"

"And if I'm not?" Jamaal asked.

"Then I hope that we can figure this thing out. I know that I want you, Jamaal, and I know that you're the one for me. I was confused for a minute but now I'm back on track and I'm ready to make things right." And I meant it. I was done with sniffing the blow, and I was done with Ron. Things had gotten too deep, and if this didn't come to an end someone was going to get hurt. I was going to tell Ron about the situation and then I would be cutting him off. If the baby did turn out to be Ron's, then he would only be a part of his child's life, not mine. Jamaal got up and walked away. I sat down at the table with my hands over my face.

A few minutes later, Jamaal came downstairs and grabbed my hand. "C'mon," he said. "You need some rest." He took me upstairs and told me to lay down. He took off my shoes and put my feet up on the bed. "Don't worry baby," he said rubbing my hair. "Tomorrow at dinner we will break the news to L.T. that he's going to have a little brother or sister but we will leave it at that. I wouldn't want to turn a happy moment for him into a sad moment."

I laid there and cried until I fell asleep.

Saturday approached, and the first thing on my list was to get over to Ron's and let him in on the news seeing as he was occupied with work on Valentine's Day, which worked out in my favor. I had made reservations for Jamaal and me at the Cheesecake Factory, and I had to admit we enjoyed our date. I hadn't felt like that in a long time. Jamaal bought me roses, candy and a Pandora bracelet. He really knew how to remind me of how lucky I was. Although things weren't at its best with Jamaal and me, he had did his best to stay calm about the whole situation. He didn't like the pregnancy dilemma, but he didn't want me to be stressed out because I was pregnant. As far as us working out our relationship, he hadn't brought it back up since the argument that we had when I revealed I was pregnant.

I pulled up to Ron's house nervous as hell. When I removed my hands from the steering wheel my palms were sweaty. After wiping them with a napkin from the glove compartment,I reached into the armrest and grabbed the hand sanitizer. As, I put the hand sanitizer back into the armrest I took a deep breath. I wasn't sure how Ron was going to feel about me being pregnant but I knew I needed to tell him. I called him to let him know that I was outside and he told me that the front door was unlocked for me to come inside. When I walked into the front door, Ron grabbed me and attempted to kiss me, but I pushed him away.

"What's wrong with you?" he asked.

"I need to talk to you," I replied as I sat down on the couch.

"About what?" Ron asked as he sat down next to me.

"I'm pregnant."

"What!" he said surprised. "By who? Your fiancé or me?"

"I don't yet."

Ron sighed. "So what you gonna do?"

"As far as the baby, I don't know because I'm not sure which one of you are the father. But as far as a relationship, I think that I wanna be with my fiance and try to save the relationship that we have worked so hard to build." I said looking Ron in the eyes.

"You what!" he yelled. "So you just gonna try and play me like that?"

"I'm not trying to play you, Ron. You knew that I was in a relationship when you met me. And I don't know why you sitting here acting like you care when you be out in the streets fucking with bitches. You must think I'm stupid." I rolled my eyes. "How many times have we set up dates and you claimed that you were busy or in the city? Then I drove by your house and your car was right outside. Didn't think I knew huh?"

"Yeah I fucked other bitches, but I ain't never treat them the way I treat you! They don't get a pair of feet every week or 14 karat bracelets!" Ron yelled.

"I never asked you for any of that shit!" I yelled back. "Everything you did was because you wanted to! I told you that I didn't need that shit! Money can't buy my love, Ronald!"

Ron shook his head. "You know what? Go ahead and go back to your fiancé if that's what you want. I can't even be mad 'cause I shouldn't have fucked with you while you had a man in the first place. I should've just fucked you and kept it moving like I was gonna do."

Tears came rolling down my face. I knew that what I did to Jamaal and Ron was wrong and although I loved the hell out of Jamaal, I did have strong feelings for Ron as well so to hear him talk to me like that really hurt my feelings. I stood up from the couch grabbing my bag. I smacked Ron in the face and started to walk toward the door. Ron jumped out of the chair and grabbed me.

"Get off of me!" I yelled.

"Come here," he said trying to pull me toward him.

"Why are you bugging?"

"Oh I'm bugging?" I asked. "You just tried to play me and I'm the one bugging?"

"I didn't mean it. I was just upset because I stopped doing a lot of shit I was doing just to make time for you and now you coming over here and telling me you're pregnant and you're not sure who the baby's father is but you wanna be with that nigga? C'mon Ni."

"At least I'm being honest with you, Ron. I'm not gonna lie, spending time with you made me start falling for you, but I hurt Jamaal. He has always been there for my son, and he's the man that my son considers his dad. L.T's not gonna accept another man in his life, and why should he have to? Jamaal's never did nothing wrong to him."

"I understand," Ron said. "So what do we do about the baby?"

"I'll keep in touch with you through the whole process. I'll call you and let you know what the sex of the baby is when I get the ultrasound done and once the baby comes and I get the blood test done we will know from there where everything stands."

"So are you saying I can't even be there for the ultrasound?"

"Like I said before, it's confusing, but Jamaal is my fiancé, so I would rather him be there. L.T. knows I'm pregnant, but he has no idea what's going on, and I don't want him to know. I'd like to keep it that way for as long as possible."

Ron shook his head. "This shit is crazy. I bet you want the baby to be Jamaal's, huh?"

"It doesn't matter what I want, Ron. Whatever God wants to happen is gonna happen."

"Yeah aight," Ron said.

"I gotta get going but I I'll be talking to you soon."

Ron looked as if he didn't want me to leave. "Can I get a hug?" he asked.

"Sure," I said reaching out for a hug.

When I got in the car, I was sad but relieved that I was able to get it out and communicate to the both of them without things getting too out of hand. I was going to go home and be with my family, something that I should have done a long time ago. The one thing that I still had on my chest and wanted to ask Jamaal was about the other woman that he had been having an affair with. Now that I had gotten my secret out, it was about time that he let me in on his. I just hoped that we could both find it in our hearts to forgive each other and move on with our lives. As I drove home, I thought about asking him about his infidelity, but I decided that I would wait a few days to give him some time to cool off.

Chapter 11

As much as I dreaded going back to work Wednesday, I had no choice. I hadn't been to work since Monday because I hadn't been feeling well. The baby had really been taking a toll on me. Jamaal had used a few of his sick days to stay at home and take care of me. Spending some alone time with each other was well needed. Jamaal had taken care of me on Monday and Tuesday while I was sick, and he promised to have dinner ready for me when I came home from work. He had been treating me like a princess and that kind of reminded me of how much of a great guy he had been to me in the past. When I got into my office, I closed my door because I didn't want to be bothered. I had started reviewing my paperwork when I heard a knock on my office door.

"Come in," I said.

My supervisor walked in with an envelope in her hand. "Good morning, Ni'raisha," she said.

"Good morning," I replied wishing that she would just give me the warning and get the hell out of my office.

She handed me the envelope. "I have to let you go," she said without even giving me an opportunity to open the envelope. "You have been missing way too many days as well as leaving early often, and we just can't tolerate that here. Your work load is becoming everyone else's problem, and it's not fair because we all have a job to do here. If I let you get away with it, then all of the other ladies are going to want to do the same."

I looked at her with a facial expression that said, "What the hell are you talking about?"

"I know that everyone gets sick or may have personal issues that need to be taken care of, but you've been missing a substantial amount of work, Ni'raisha, and in order to keep our company running successfully, we need to have reliable individuals working here. Having an employee that never comes to work means the job doesn't get done in a timely manner."

There was nothing I could say to defend myself. She was right. Ever since I had gotten involved with Ron I had been missing a lot of work. I stood up at my desk. "I understand," I said as I dug under the desk grabbing an empty box to pack my things in. Deep down inside I was horrified. What was I going to tell Jamaal?

"I hope that you can understand my decision to let you go."

"I do," I said.

"Here's your last check, and although today is your last day we paid for you for the rest of the week," she said handing me a sealed payroll envelope. "I'm sorry." She walked out of the room closing the door behind her.

I finished packing up my things, and without a goodbye I walked past the receptionist desk and out of that door for the last time.

On my way home, I was thinking of what I would tell Jamaal. He would never understand me getting fired for my attendance. The discharge letter clearly stated that I had incurred a large amount of absences as well as repeatedly shortening my work days. He would wonder where I had been since I hadn't been to work and this could really take a strain in our relationship. He would definitely figure out that I was with Ron, and the thought of me losing my job because I chose to spend time with another man would probably not sit well with him. I would just have to tell him that I got laid off.

When I pulled up to the house, Jamaal's car was outside. I was hoping that he had stepped out for a bit because I was so nervous about telling him. I took a deep breath and braced myself to go inside and break the news to him. I walked into the living room where the TV had been on but Jamaal was not in there. "Why did he leave this TV on?" I said as I grabbed the remote and turned the power off on the TV I made my way up the stairs.

As I reached the top of the stairs, I noticed that the bedroom door had been closed and I could hear moaning coming from the bedroom. Without hesitation, I forced the bedroom door open, and there was Jamaal on top of another woman. He jumped up in surprise and what I saw next was a travesty.

The woman in my bed was Natty!

I ran downstairs and headed for the kitchen drawer. Jamaal came running down behind me. I grabbed a knife out of the drawer and charged toward him. He grabbed my hand and tried to take the knife from me. "Ni, you're pregnant! Calm down!"

"How could you!" I yelled. "She was my friend!"

Natty came walking down the stairs buttoning her blouse. I charged at her, and Jamaal grabbed me. "So this is why you were acting funny, bitch! Because you've been fucking my fiancé! I bet you're the one that told him about Ron, huh?"

I charged at her again. Jamaal repeatedly grabbed me as I charged at Natty.

"You were the one that fucked up Ni, so why are you blaming me for everything that happened!"

"What I did has nothing to do with it! The issue at hand is you fucking my fiancé, bitch!" I screamed.

"He's not your fiancé anymore, remember? You don't even know who that baby's daddy is, and if you really loved Jamaal you would've never fucked another nigga, period!"

I grabbed a plate out of the dish rack and lunged it at her head. She ducked to avoid the plate hitting her. "I'm gonna fuck you up, bitch!" I yelled at her.

"Ni baby listen, calm down." Jamaal said.

"Calm down my ass!" I yelled.

"You just better thank God you ain't dead yet!" Natty interrupted.

"Ni I love you like a sister. You, Tay and I have been friends since high school, but I just don't think that you deserve Jamaal, and I never did. You deserved Mark, and I deserve Jamaal. Jamaal deserves someone who's gonna be true to him and be there for him when he really needs them."

"C'mon chill with all that," Jamaal said to Natty.

"And this is coming from someone who couldn't satisfy her man and that's why he went elsewhere?" I said.

Natty's eyes filled up with tears and she and she lunged at me. Jamaal pushed Natty away. "Yo, just go!" he yelled at Natty.

"Go for what? Why do I have to go? This is your house!"

"And this is my fiancé! Now go!" Jamaal screamed.

Natty stormed out of the door with anger in her eyes slamming the door behind her. I pushed Jamaal out of the way and went upstairs to pack some things for L.T. and I.

"Where you going Ni?" Jamaal said as he came running up the stairs.

"Get the fuck away from me!" I yelled as I burst out in tears.

"Just relax and stop stressing yourself out! It's not good for the baby!" he said.

"Relax? I just caught my fucking fiancé in bed with one of my best friends and you want me to relax!" I said as I shoved some clothes into a duffle bag. "Of all the females in the fucking world, you had to go and fuck my friend!" I started walking down the stairs.

"Ni, where you going?" Jamaal asked.

"Don't worry about it," I said.

"Where are you taking L.T?" he asked.

"To my mom's," I answered.

"So you just gonna drop L.T. off and go run to that nigga huh?"

"Don't worry about me, Jamaal," I said.

"You just keep on fucking Natty."

"Oh c'mon, Ni! It was a mistake! You made a mistake! A big fucking mistake, and I'm still here with you!"

"First of all my baby is not a mistake and secondly I may have fucked up but I would never had fucked one of your friends!" I said as I brushed past Jamaal.

I slammed the door behind me. When I got into the car I could see Jamaal standing at the door with tears in his eyes. I sped off as if I were in a hurry. I picked up the phone and called Ron.

"What happened?" he asked. "You changed your mind?"

"I'm just going through something right now, Ron. Is it okay if I come and stay with you for a while? This is temporary just until I can get my own place."

"Of course," Ron said. "You know I'm not gonna leave you in the streets and you pregnant. What about your little man?"

"He's going to stay with my mom for a bit. He will be fine."

"Are you sure 'cause he can come too if you want him to? I can grab a futon for the living room."

"No, he will be fine with my mom. I just don't want to confuse him."

"No that's cool. I respect that," Ron said.

"Thanks," I said.

"Well come on over. I'll be waiting for you."

"Alright. I'll see you in a few."

After we hung up, I picked up the phone and called my mom to explain the situation. She didn't know everything that was going on but had agreed to keep L.T. until I got back on my feet or in her hopes, at least until Jamaal and I worked things out. L.T. was her baby and she not going to let him endure all of the drama that was taking place with us. I pulled up to L.T.'s school.

"Hey Mom," L.T. said as he hopped into the back seat of the car.

"Hey baby," I replied. "How did your day go at school?"

"It went good. You didn't go to work today?"

"Yes, I went to work. I got laid off today, baby."

"Oh," he said glancing at the two duffel bags in the back seat. "Ma what are those bags for?"

My phone rang and it was Jamaal. I forwarded him to voicemail. "You are going to go and stay at grandma's house for a little while."

L.T. put his head down. "Are you and daddy breaking up?"

"Baby, Jamaal and I just have some things that we need to figure out."

L.T. started to cry. "I knew that you guys were breaking up. That's why everyone's been acting different. You guys don't even hug and kiss like you use to."

I pulled the car over to the side of the road. I turned to L.T. in the passenger seat. "L.T. listen, sometimes things don't always work out the way that we want then to, but that doesn't mean that daddy and I don't love you. I don't know if your dad and I are going to be together, and sometimes it's for the best. Would you rather see Jamaal and me running around the house arguing or would you rather see us communicating as good friends? The three of us can still go out and do things together."

Although I was not sure if this was true, my baby was hurting at the moment and I had to say something to convince him that everything would be okay.

L.T. looked up at me with his lips poked out. "So you two will still be friends?"

I nodded. "For now and if it is meant for daddy and I to work things out then we will okay?"

"Okay," L.T. said nodding in agreement. I kissed him on the forehead and put my seatbelt on. "Are you hungry?"

"Yeah," L.T. replied.

.

We went to eat at the Steakhouse then I dropped L.T. off at my mom's house. After talking with my mom for a bit I called L.T. back into the living room. I gave him a big hug and a kiss. "I will give you a call later on tonight baby and you make sure that you behave for grandma."

"I will," L.T. said holding me as if he did not want to let go. I gave my mom a kiss on the cheek and headed over to Ron's.

When I arrived at Ron's house, he came out and grabbed my bag for me. Ron did me the favor of unpacking my bag for me and placing my clothes in a few empty dressers that he had made available for me. "Are you hungry?" he asked me.

"No, I'm fine. I just ate at the steak house with my little man."

"Alright well I gotta hit the block to check on these niggas and make sure my money straight but I'll be back in a few hours. Make yourself at home," he said smiling.

"Alright," I said smiling back. I was just happy that he hadn't asked me what happened. Maybe he just didn't care to know but whatever the case had been I was okay with that. I walked into the bedroom and grabbed my cell phone out of my handbag. I had nine missed calls from Jamaal and seven messages. I deleted every last message without even listening to them. Although I had told L.T. that Jamaal and I might get back together, I knew that there was absolutely no chance of that happening. He had crossed the line, and there was no way his actions could be forgiven. I was so angry at the moment that I had no intention of ever even speaking to him again but one thing was for sure, I did have intentions of whooping on Natty's ass when I caught her.

I peeked out of the living room window to make sure that Ron's car was gone. I went into my contacts list and called Tay.

Tay picked up. "Well hello, Ni, and why didn't I hear from you on Sunday?"

"I know I was supposed to go to church with you, and I'm sorry that I couldn't make it, but right now I need to hear some of the good Lord's words."

"Okay girl, what happened now?" Tay asked.

"Tay, brace yourself for this one. Can you believe that I walked in my house and caught Jamaal in bed with Natty?"

"What! Our friend Natty!"

"Yep," I answered. The thought of it brought tears running down my face.

"Ni, are you serious?"

"Yes Tay, I'm serious," I replied.

"So that's why she was getting all hostile with you on the phone," Tay said. "All this time she was sleeping around with Jamaal? She's just a few months too late. If I weren't saved, I'd kick her butt for you."

"Oh, I tried but Jamaal kept holding me. I was about to stab him if he didn't grab that damn knife from me," I said.

"Where's Jamaal at right now?" Tay asked.

"He's at home, I guess. I'm at Ron's house, and I'm gonna be staying here for a while. I had to get away from him because I probably would have killed his ass."

"And where's L.T?"

"I bought him to my mom's house to stay for a bit until I get this whole thing figured out." "So was Natty still at the house with Jamaal when you left?"

"Hell no! Jamaal made her ass leave and now he's calling me leaving all of these messages that I really don't care to hear."

"Yes girl. He definitely went overboard with that. I mean come on now. Jamaal knew that you, me and Natty are very close friends."

"Was," I corrected Tay.

"Yeah you're right," Tay said. "She was supposed to be a friend so no matter what that never should have happened and I'm guessing that she was the one who told Jamaal about you and Ron."

"Yeah she did and I don't have any words for her. I'm not trying to hear nothing about how she was so heartbroken from her divorce and needed someone to talk to."

"You ain't the only one," Tay replied. "I'm through with her, too, and she better not call me because I'm going to let her have it. I'm going to express my true feelings to her and I'm not holding nothing back either."

"Tay, today has just been a bad day overall. I lost my damn job today, too."

"Now how did that happen Ni?"

"That was my own fault," I answered. "When I first started getting caught up with Ron, I was missing a lot of work. My supervisor had given me warnings but I had appointments that I had to make as well that I couldn't cancel so I would have to leave work early. She said that she had to let me go because they could not continue to try and maintain their work load and mine at the same time."

"Oh girl, you gotta get to church and ask God for forgiveness because your life is just in shambles right now."

"You are absolutely right about that," I said.

"So does that meant that you will be going to church with me this Sunday?" Tay asked.

"Yeah. I'll go," I replied.

"Good. Also, I wanted to tell you that I am picking up my keys for my new place on

Friday, and I want you to come with me over there so that you can check it out. Besides, I want you to help me with the decorating. It'll help get your mind off of all of the things that you're going through."

"Okay. That sounds good," I said. "So what time on Friday are we going?"

"I'm going to meet the landlord at 5:30, so if you can just meet me at my house at about 5:15 that would be cool."

"Okay. Sounds like a plan to me girl."

"Alright. You go and get some rest and I'm about to finish doing some packing. Then I'm going to relax and watch me some TV."

"Okay Tay. I'll talk to you later."

"And if things don't work out where you're at you are more than welcome to come and stay with me until you get on your feet," she said.

"Thanks a lot Tay," I replied.

"Yep. I will talk to you soon."

"Okay." Click.

When Ron came home, he laid down on the bed next to me and pulled out his aluminum foil. I knew what time it was. As bad as I had wanted to take a few hits, I knew that it was not safe for the baby, so I decided against it. If I were going to try and make my life better for me, L.T, and the baby then I needed to start now.

"Ron?" I said.

"Yes baby," he answered.

"Can you not do that shit around me? I mean I would actually prefer if you stop doing it all together because it would really help me, but if you feel that you can't help but to do it can you at least go in the bathroom?"

"Well I'll go in the bathroom, but it's not that easy to just stop. You don't have a choice right now. You know I'm not about to let you do it 'cause you pregnant, but shit, I'm good. I'm not the one that's pregnant and I been doing this shit for eight years, so what makes you think I'm gonna just stop now because you want me to?"

I looked at him and rolled my eyes. How could I have not known that this man was on drugs? If I had known, Jamaal and I might still be together because I would have never gotten involved with him.

Ron stood up from the bed. "Who the fuck are you looking at like that?"

I stood silent.

"Yeah that's what the fuck I thought," he said as he went walking into the living room.

I knew that I wouldn't be there too long. My first day there and he was already showing signs of control and violence. I felt like he was only acting out because he knew that I was desperate at the moment. Knowing that Jamaal and I were going through something and I needed him made him feel like he was some kind of hero. If things got too bad, I would just go to stay at Tay's house. I really did not want to impose on her and especially since she was finally gaining her independence. My mom loved me but she probably wouldn't allow me back into her house at this point especially since she wanted me and Jamaal to work things out. She would probably figure if she allowed me to stay there then there would be no chance of Jamaal and I getting back together. She felt like everything that happened was my fault, and she loved Jamaal to death. When it came to her grandchild there was nothing to talk about. She would never leave L.T. out on the streets.

After I had dropped off L.T., I left my mom's house full of thought. She had told me that she hoped Ron was worth losing my family and had blamed him for everything as well. She had always been tough on me growing up seeing as I was an only child. I use to think that she had felt some kind of hatred for me deep down, but I wasn't sure if she intentionally meant to be harsh on me or if maybe she just couldn't see that she was treating me like a step child. Maybe my mom and my dad separating added to it. Everyone would always say I was a replicate of my dad. Lucky for me, I had my best friend, Tay. She and L.T. were my only family that I could count on.

Chapter 12

Saturday had consisted of a day full of nausea, fatigue, and a headache that jus would not go away so I practically slept throughout the entire day. Later that night, I had been asleep when my phone rang. Without looking at the caller ID, I forwarded it to voicemail. I assumed that it was probably Jamaal calling me again because he had been calling all day. Not even a minute later, my phone rang again, and this time I checked the caller ID. The number was not familiar to me so I forwarded it a second time thinking that Jamaal was trying to pull a fast one on me by calling from an unknown number. The phone immediately started ringing again from that same number, so I figured it had to be important and decided to take the call.

"Hello," I answered.

"Hi Ni'raisha?"

"Speaking." I said not recognizing the caller's voice.

"This is Tayla's mom," she said.

"Oh hello Mrs. Lanes." I said. As I sat up in the bed and turned on the lamp that sat on the nightstand, I knew that if Tay's mom had been calling me late at night repeatedly then something was definitely wrong. Before I could ask her how she was doing, she interrupted me. "Ni'raisha, Tayla passed away tonight," Mrs. Lanes said as she broke down crying.

"What!" I said screaming out loud. I began crying out loud.

Ron came running into the room to see what was wrong with me. "Are you okay?" he asked.

Ignoring him I asked Tay's mom what had happened. "She got stabbed by some girl that was fooling around with that no good boy, Ty. I told Tayla that boy was no good for her when I first met him. I just wished that she would've have listened to me."

"Well where was she?" I asked.

"She was on her way home from Bible study, and she stopped at the diner on Washington Avenue to grab something to eat. The police said according to witnesses the girl had approached Tayla as she was walking out of the diner. They started exchanging words and she just stabbed my baby." Tay's mother broke down crying again. "My baby's gone all because of some low-life bastard! I'm not supposed to outlive my child, she was supposed to outlive me!"

"I'm so sorry Mrs. Lanes. Did they at least catch the girl that stabbed her?" I asked, knowing that it was Ty's long-time fling that me and Tay had given the business to at club Lusion.

"They caught her. She's in jail, and I hope she rots in there."

I tried to calm myself because I knew that I needed to be strong for Tay's mom at the moment. "How many times did she get stabbed?"

"Three times, but one of them pierced an artery, and that's what killed her. I just can't believe my baby's gone. She was trying so hard to change her life around."

"I know," I said. "Mrs. Lanes, would it be okay if I came by and saw you tomorrow?"

"Sure baby, anytime. You were Tayla's best friend, and you two have always been so close growing up. I know that I will have to find the strength to go and clean out her place, but at this moment I just don't think that I can do it, Ni'raisha." She continued to cry into the receiver.

"Well if you want me to go with you I can definitely go. I would actually love to go with you if you will allow me to." I said.

"No, it's okay, Ni'raisha. Tayla told me that you were pregnant, and I don't want you stress yourself too much. It's not good for the baby."

All I could think about was that Tay was going to be my baby's godmother and now she would never even get to meet her godchild. Tears uncontrollably rolled down my face.

Ron stood in front of me looking at me and trying to figure out what exactly was going on.

"Mrs. Lanes, it's really not a problem. I will be okay."

"Okay well thank you so much, Ni'raisha, and I guess tomorrow when you come by we can figure out what day works best for the both of us to go over there," she said.

"Alright so I will give you a call tomorrow before I head over," I said.

"Okay sweetie," she replied.

After we hung up the phone, I broke down crying again. Ron grabbed me in his arms and asked me what happened. I couldn't stop crying enough to tell him what happened.

"Calm down Ni. Look at me," he said grabbing my face and turning it toward him. He gave me a minute to calm down and then he asked me again. "Now what happened, baby?"

"My best friend got killed."

"Who? Homegirl that was with you at the mall the day I met you?"

I nodded.

"Damn. How'd she get killed?" Ron asked.

"Some fucking chick that she was beefing with over her ex stabbed her," I said with anger in my eyes.

"Word?" he said turning his head. "That's some crazy shit."

"I'm going to see her mom tomorrow; I can't even begin to imagine what she's feeling," I said shaking my head.

"C'mon," Ron said grabbing my arm. "You need to lay down and get some rest. I'm sorry about what happened to your girl and I know that this is gonna be hard for you to deal with but try not to stress too much 'cause it's not good for the baby aight?"

I nodded and laid down in the bed. Ron laid down in the bed beside me with his hand over my stomach. I couldn't believe that this was happening to me. My best friend from high school was gone, and she was never coming back. She was the only true friend that I had besides Natty, who turned out to be a foe. The chick did promise to return the favor of the beatdown that we had given her, but why did she have to kill her? I didn't know how I was going to make it without her. I no longer had someone by my side that I could talk to and that wouldn't judge me. What in the hell was I going to do now? I knew that had I been with Jamaal he would have been there for me. He had always been my support system and been there for me when I needed him. Tay and Jamaal were the two people in my life who knew exactly what to say to make things better. I lied in the bed crying all night.

Chapter 14

Two months had passed, and although I didn't want to, I had been forcing myself to getting used to not having Tay around. She had looked so beautiful and peaceful in her casket, and I tried to convince myself that she was sleeping and happy where she was at. Everybody had shown up at her funeral to pay their respects, including Natty, Jamaal, and even Mark which was a surprise to me. Although I had still wanted to punch Natty in the face, it was Tay's funeral, and I knew that it was neither the time nor the place for it. She couldn't even look me in the face. "What a fucking coward," I thought to myself. After the funeral, Jamaal had approached me and wanted to know how things were going with me and the baby.

"We are fine," I said. Thank you for asking."

"Your stomach is getting big," Jamaal said glancing down at it.

"I know. She is going to be a big girl." I replied.

Jamaal's eyes widened. "Wow. A little girl huh?" he said with a slight smile on his face.

"Yep," I replied rubbing my belly. "I just can't wait until October because this baby is kicking my butt."

Jamaal laughed. "Hey did L.T. tell you about the basketball game I took him to a few weeks ago?"

"Yeah, he told me that you two go out a few times a week to eat and hang out. Thank you for still being a part of his life."

"No problem Ni. That's still my little man regardless of what happened between us. Maybe you should come and hang out with us sometime you know? This will show L.T. that we are both mature and cordial about the situation."

"I don't know," I shook my head. "I'm going to have to get back to you on that one."

"Okay cool," Jamaal said as nodding. "I'm sorry about what happened to Tay. I'm really gonna miss her crazy self."

"Thanks for coming," I replied.

"You're welcome. So do you need anything or are you good?"

"No, I'm okay but thanks for asking."

"Well my number hasn't changed so you can give me a call anytime you need something."

Curious as to whether he was still fooling around with Natty I said, "Hmmm. Are you sure that's going to be okay with Natty?"

Jamaal put his head down. "Ni', I don't deal with her anymore. I haven't slept with that girl since the day you caught us. I know I was wrong, and I know I fucked up, but I think that I was really vulnerable at that time. Finding out that you had been sleeping around with another man when I had been faithful to you our whole relationship? Then you telling me that you were pregnant but you weren't sure who the father was? What man wants to hear some shit like that from his soon-to-be wife? I guess I was just so hurt that I felt like doing something that would hurt you would make me feel better and make us even."

I began to tear up. "I was wrong, and I'm sorry for hurting you."

I wiped the tears from my face. "Once again, I apologize, Ni, and I hope that you will consider hanging out with me and L.T. sometime."

I nodded. "I'll think about it, and I will give you a call." I turned and started to walk away. It was so hard for me to see Jamaal and not wanna be with him but I think we both knew that things could never be the same.

Things with Ron and I were going well considering he was highly addicted to the coke. I knew that I wasn't as happy as I would have liked to be but at this point I had no choice but to make things work because I needed to have a roof over my head. He had been so excited to find out the sex of the baby that he hoped was his. Since he had found out the sex of the baby, he made it his business to go with me to every appointment. After seeing Jamaal, I felt kind of bad that I had not invited him to come along with me to any of my appointments, but I knew that there was no way in hell Ron was going for that.

I had been having a lot of fatigue with the pregnancy, and at four months I would have thought that the symptoms would have vanished by now. The night before I had even come down with a fever and I had to have Ron run out and grab me some Tylenol. My pregnancy with L.T. had been a breeze, but I reminded myself that the chances of me being lucky enough to have a smooth pregnancy with this one were slim to none. One thing was for sure, October 17 would be the happiest day of my life. Not only would I not have to endure any more of the fatigue, emotions, and side effects of being pregnant, but I would finally get to meet my bundle of joy. After checking my blood pressure and advising me that it was fine, Dr. Winn decided that I would need to have more blood work drawn to eliminate anything serious. When Ron and I left the doctor's office, we stopped at Duchess to get something to eat and then we headed home. L.T's birthday was coming up so I gave him a call at my mom's house to let him know that I didn't forget his birthday and that I would be stopping by to see him.

"Hey Mom!" he said excitedly.

"Hi baby," I replied.

"What are you doing?"

"I'm about to go shopping with dad. Do you wanna come?"

"No thanks, hun. Mommy's tired."

"When are you having the baby?"

"In October," I answered.

"Mom, dad's here!" L.T. screamed.

"Okay baby well look, you go ahead and go out with dad and I will give you a call tomorrow." I said, ending the call assuring him that I loved him.

I went into the living room and started watching TV Things were much more different from being with Jamaal. Ron was never home and I was always stuck in the house alone. He would never just walk in the house and kiss me the way that Jamaal did. As the days went by, I was seeing less and less of him and I was starting to feel like I was just a pregnant chick who was only good for sex. I was grateful that he at least made sure that he went with me to the doctors but he was giving me the perception that he really didn't even want to be bothered with me but only wanted me around because of the baby.

A few days had gone by since my appointment with Dr. Winn and I had gotten a call from one of the nurses saying that Dr. Winn would like for me to come in to discuss the results of the blood work. I was nervous as hell but had hoped that it was nothing too serious. I picked up the phone and dialed Ron's cell phone.

"Yo," he answered.

"Hey I just got a call from the doctor's office. My blood work is back and Dr. Winn wants me to come in to discuss the results. Are you going to come with me?"

"Nah. It's booming out here today. I gotta stay out here and get this money but you go ahead and I will see you later when I get home."

"Alright," I said hanging up without saying goodbye. This street shit was really becoming a little too much for me and as soon as I got myself together, I intended on leaving his ass. Seeming as I was always cramped up in that damn house alone, there was really no reason for me to be there. I grabbed my keys and my handbag and headed out of the door.

When I arrived at the doctor's office, Dr. Winn called me into the room and closed the door behind her. "How are we feeling today?" she asked.

"Could be better," I said smiling.

"I'm sorry to hear that," she said as she took a seat in the chair across from me. "I got the results of your blood work back. I don't know how to tell you this...you tested positive for H.I.V."

My face dropped and my eyes widened. "Are you sure, Dr. Winn?"

"As much I would hate to be wrong, the test is more than 99.5 percent accurate."

"Can I be tested again just to be sure?" I asked petrified and still in denial.

"The test has been run twice just to be sure that you receive accurate information," she assured me.

Unsure of what to do I just sat there with a blank look on my face.

"At this point, what I can do for you is prescribe you some antiretroviral medicines that will assist in protecting the baby from contracting H.I.V. Did you want to go ahead and start on those meds?"

I nodded and continued to stare into space. So many thoughts were running through my head. How could Ron do this to me? What if I passed it on to Jamaal? Will I live to see my children have children?

Dr. Winn pretended to clear her throat to get my attention. "If you would like counseling to help you cope with this, I can type you up a referral."

"No. I'm okay for now," I said.

"Okay well here are you prescriptions that you will need to take in addition to your prenatal vitamins," she said as she filled each prescription out and handed them to me.

"Thanks," I said as I stood up from my chair.

"And Ni'raisha don't forget, anytime you feel that you are ready for counseling you can just give us a call."

"Will do," I said as I walked out of the door. I drove the whole way home in silence.

The only thing on my mind was killing Ron but I knew that would take me away from my kids quicker than this virus.

It was 10 o' clock at night and Ron had walked in the house smelling like a pound of weed and a liquor store. I was on the bed with an angry look on my face.

"What's wrong with you?" Ron asked.

"Is there something that you wanna tell me?" I asked him.

"Something like what?"

"Are you H.I.V positive, Ron?"

"Nah. Why you ask me that?"

"Because when I went to my appointment today I found out that I'm fucking H.I.V positive!" I yelled as I started crying.

"Calm down, Ni," Ron said as he grabbed me and started to rub my back.

I looked up at him. "You knew you were positive didn't you?"

"C'mon now, Ni," Ron said.

I interrupted him, "You knew you were positive 'cause you are awfully fucking calm for someone who just found out they're gonna die!" I screamed.

"It ain't shit we can do at this point, so what the fuck we gon do cry about it! It's not gonna change the situation, Ni!"

"What about my fucking kids, huh Ron? Did you even consider the fact that I had a fucking child that existed when I met you! What about my little boy that might graduate from high school and not even have his mother there for one of the most greatest moments of his life! What about my little girl who can possibly be born with the disease! That doesn't matter to you does it!"

"What the fuck are you yelling at me like that for? You're the one who opened your fucking legs to me without protection, so it's just as much your fault that you got that shit as it is mine!"

I broke down crying. "Fuck you, Ron! I should have your ass arrested!"

Ron grabbed me by my throat and threw me down on the bed. "Bitch, don't you ever fucking threaten me like that again, or I will fucking kill you! You understand me?"

Knowing that I had nowhere else to go and I needed Ron I shook my head yes. Ron released his hand from around my neck and stormed out of the house slamming the door behind him. I laid on the bed crying and trying to figure out why Ron was trying to make me feel like I was the one who did something wrong. It was obvious that he had given me the virus because he never denied it but the thing that really hurt me was that he had no intentions on telling me, nor did he show any remorse for what he had done to me. I laid there motionless and in another world. If there was a time that I really needed Tay, that time would have been now. I couldn't understand why god was punishing me like this. I started to question if there really was a god and if there was then I wanted answers. On the other hand, it was more than obvious that I had brought this on myself and I would just have to accept and learn to cope with everything that was happening to me.

Chapter 14

At about 3 o'clock in the morning, I awoke to what I thought had been banging on the door. Before I could get out of the bed there had been task force agents everywhere. They had grabbed Ron out of bed and thrown him to the floor. The officers had their guns out yelling for me to put my hands up. They proceeded to open the closet doors and did a quick sweep of the rest of the house. Two of the officers cuffed Ron and read him his Miranda rights. As they exited the house with Ron, they demanded that I step out of the house so that they can perform a full search of the apartment. There were cars everywhere and that was all they needed to bring the whole neighborhood out. I put my head down trying to avoid looking at any of the nosey ass neighbors. An officer approached me with a notepad and asked me for my name and identification.

"My driver's license is in the house in my bag," I said aware that he probably already knew this.

"Is there anything in that house that we should know about?" he asked.

"Not that I am aware of."

I wasn't worried about them finding anything in the house because Ron never kept drugs in the house unless it was drugs that he used for his own personal high. Once he bagged everything up he would usually hand it off to his workers right away,. I could only hope that he had sniffed up any coke that he had in the house. One of the officers came out of the house with plastic bags and one of the officers was talking to another officer while placing a Glock 9mm in a brown paper bag. What the fuck! What the fuck was Ron thinking? Those fucking drugs must have been getting to his head because Ron would have never been stupid enough to have drugs or guns up in the house. He knew the rules of the game, and if he slipped up then I was not going down with him.

The officer approached me. "So you didn't know that your boyfriend had drugs and weapons in there?" he said pointing to the house.

"Officer I swear I had no idea," I replied.

Another officer interrupted, "You do know that we can take you in, too, don't you?"

"Yes, I am aware of that, but I really had no idea that there was anything in there. I am not lying," I said with a sincere look on my face.

"When we finish up here you can go ahead and go back inside and for future references you should really check the background of the guys you decide to date," one of the officers' said. In my head I was saying, "And who the fuck are you?" but the only words that came out of my mouth were, "Yes sir."

When the officers left and the coast was clear, I walked into the house and sat down in the living room. I sat there on the couch not knowing what I would do next. I had no job, no money, and nowhere to go. The rent was paid up for the month but a new month was approaching in less than two weeks. Although my mom and I did not click the way that a mother and daughter were supposed to, I decided to give it a shot at asking her if I can come and stay with her. At this point in my life, it couldn't get any worse than what it already was so even if she did say no I would just have to suck it up and think of my next move. Hopefully she wouldn't be so heartless to turn me down and leave me on the streets while I was pregnant. Then again she knew that I had nowhere to go when Jamaal and I first separated and she didn't offer for me to come and stay at her place. It was late so I would just have to wait until tomorrow to call her. I had to figure something out. All of the emotions that I was going through wasn't healthy for the baby. The only thing I could do was pray on it now. A couple of hours had passed and I must have cried so much that I had cried myself to sleep.

The phone rang, and it was Ron calling from police department. "Yo Ni, call this number and ask for Rock. Let him know that I'm locked up and my bail is $75,000. See if he can hold me down until I get up out of here. With a bondsmen, he should only need about seventy hundred, maybe even less. Let him know that the boys raided the block and they got all these niggas up in here so he's the only one I really got right now."

"Well what if he say that he ain't got it?" I asked.

"Trust me, he got it but if he try and front on me then I'm gonna need you to try and see if you can get this money up for me. They took all the money I had."

I knew that with all of the money he had been making that was impossible. I figure it could probably be one of three things. Either he didn't want to talk over the phone about the whereabouts of his dough, or maybe he didn't trust me enough because he had never mentioned anything to me about any money that he had hidden around. Maybe he had his money at some bitch's house that he was fucking and trusted and now that his ass was locked up she wasn't coming up off his money. She probably figured if he couldn't get bonded out he was gonna be stuck in the pen doing time. By the time he got out she would be somewhere long gone with all of his damn money. If that was the case, then Ron got everything that he deserved. I would hope that if there was any one he would leave money around or advise of a hidden stash, it would be me considering I was possibly carrying his child.

Ron interrupted my thoughts, "Ni! Do you hear me?"

"Yes I heard you Ron," I lied. "Where am I supposed to get this money from if your homeboy don't come through? You know I ain't got nobody and even if I did ain't nobody about to let me borrow that kind of money."

"Just make it happen. How long have I been taking care of your ass and I ain't never ask you for nothing? I'm telling you right now, Ni, if you can't look out for me and if I do end up getting out of here, you can't ask me for shit. I don't care if that is my baby."

"Well I didn't ask you for what I got now," I said referring to my disease.

Yo, not right now Ni," he said. "Just call Rock and see what's up and if he say he can't do it then see what you can do for me."

"Aight," I said not really caring whether he stayed in there or got out at this point. The only reason that I was with him was because I had no one and nowhere else to turn to. He had made my life a living hell. Thanks to Ron my life had been all fucked up. In my eyes, I was a pregnant low-life living with H.I.V and a drug dealer who was never home but somehow seemed to think that he was in control of me because I was on my last leg. On top of that I still had to figure out how I was going to break the news to Jamaal. It was only fair that I told him so that he could go and get tested.

I picked up the phone and dialed the number that Ron had given me.

A guy picked up the phone.

"Hello, is this Rock?" I asked.

"Who is this?" the guy on the other end asked.

"My name is Ni. I'm Ron's girlfriend."

He chuckled. "Which one?"

I thought to myself, "Damn this nigga is rude," but I decided to overlook his smart ass remark. "Ron got locked up and his bond his $75,000, so he told me to call and ask you if you can help him get out. He said that he will pay you back when he get out."

He started laughing "This is a joke right?"

"No," I said confused as to why he was laughing. This jerk was really beginning to piss me off now. "What's so funny?" I asked.

"What's so fucking funny is that I haven't heard from this nigga in like a year and now he needs me to do him a favor?"

"Pretty much," I replied not sure of what else to say. "Let me tell you something," he said.

"You tell that nigga that I said I got it, but he ain't getting it. He wanted to go out there and try to be the big man. I didn't care about him not wanting to fuck with me on that level, but that shit shouldn't have kept us from being cool. Shit, I practically raised your man. Shit, we was good up until a year ago when he started getting money and his head got big."

I had had enough of his little autobiography of him and Ron's history. "Okay. Enough said."

"Yo and make sure that you tell him I said that, too," he said.

"Alright," I said.

"You sound sexy, shorty. How long you been dealing with that lame?"

I ignored him. "I will give Ron the message when he calls me."

"Damn you ain't gotta be all uptight. Shit, I just figured now that your boo is gon you might wanna come fuck with a real nigga. I don't know how Ron had you living, but it ain't nothing but the good life over here, baby."

"Excuse me? I am pregnant with Ron's child and I have no intentions of getting involved with one of his boys."

"Don't they say that's the best?" He laughed.

I knew exactly what he was referring to. "Okay. It was nice talking to you and goodbye."

"Ay hold up," he said.

"Yes? I said thinking that maybe he had changed his mind about not helping Ron out.

"You got my number, so maybe you should use it sometime."

I hung up on him without a response. I walked into the room and laid down on the bed. I was so exhausted and worn out but it was obvious shit just wasn't going to get any better unless I took the necessary steps to it better.

Unfortunately for me, I just wasn't sure where to start. I had awakening the next morning feeling more depressed than I had ever felt in my life. The thought that I was going to die from AIDs never left my mind. It had me contemplating suicide but the fact that it would not be fair to L.T. or the new baby, made me change my mind. I just hoped that the baby would not be affected by it. The only person that I had to possibly help me through this was my mom, but I had not even told her about my condition yet. In fact, I had told no one afraid of what they would think of me but I knew that I would eventually have to say something. There was a knock at the door, and I got up to answer it.

It was an older black lady with grey hair at the door. "Is Ronald available?" she asked.

"He's not here at the moment," I said.

"Well who are you?" she asked.

"I'm a friend," I replied. "And you?"

"I'm the landlord," she said with a smart expression on her face. I received a call from a source telling me that some action had taken place here in the middle of the night, so I'm guessing Mr. Richmond is incarcerated, huh?" She tried to sneak a peek inside of the house.

"Yes he is," I replied.

"One thing that I will not allow is a drug dealer for a tenant," she said.

I looked at her dumbfounded.

"Have you been staying here?" she asked me.

I didn't know what to say. "I'm here visiting from Virginia," I said. "Ronald was nice enough to let me stay here doing my visit."

The look on her face told me that she knew I was lying. "Well young lady, you are not on the lease, and if Mr. Richmond wasn't in jail I would be serving him with an eviction notice right about now, but since that is not the case I guess he saved me the trouble. I'm going to have to ask you to get your things and leave."

"Now?" I asked.

"I'm a pretty fair person, so I will give you until the end of the day. You will have to be out of here no later than midnight. After that, I'm going to have to call the cops to have you escorted off of the premises."

"That won't be necessary," I said. "I'll be out of here in a couple of hours. I just need to get my things together."

"Thank you," she said as she turned and started walking away. As I attempted to close the door behind her, I heard her yell out to me. "Uh Miss."

"Yes," I said swinging the door back open. "You wouldn't happen to have a key would you?"

"No, I don't." I answered.

"Okay thanks," she said and continued to walk to her car. I closed the door and walked into the living room to sit down. I picked up my cell phone and called my mom.

"Hello," she answered. "Hi mom," I said. "Oh hey."

"Where's L.T?" I asked.

"He went to play basketball with the neighbor's son." Now that I knew L.T. wasn't around I needed to get straight to the point. "Mom I have to tell you something."

"What did you get yourself into now?" she asked.

At that moment, I thought about not saying anything because she had always criticized me for everything I've ever done but at this point it really didn't matter anymore. "Mom I'm H.I.V positive," I said holding in my tears.

"What!" she yelled.

"Mom before you start criticizing me about this let me just say that I am going through enough dealing with this and it would be great if you for once support me rather than judge me on decisions that I've made in my life."

She became calm. "Well how did this happen? It was that little thug you were messing around with wasn't it?"

"Yes," I answered now wanting to change the subject.

"You do realize that you brought this all on yourself, Ni'raisha."

"Yes mom, I know but we all make mistakes and the important thing is that we learn from them."

"Hmmm, if you had learned from your mistake then you wouldn't be living with him now and especially since he is the one that infected you. Does Jamaal know about this?"

"No, and don't tell him anything because I wanna tell him face to face. I want him to go and get tested as well."

"Well you need to tell him as soon as possible. And I don't know how you are going to explain this to L.T."

"Mom, let me just take things one step at a time. I'm going to tell Jamaal and L.T. but first I have to get myself situated."

"Situated how?" she asked.

"I need a place to stay."

"What's going on? Thing's not going to well with you and your man?"

I thought about lying and just telling my mom that I was just ready to leave him but knowing that things couldn't get any worse I decided to give her the truth. "Ron got locked up, and I have to be out of here today by midnight."

"So where are you gonna go?

"I was actually calling you to see if I can possibly come and stay with you until I can get myself together."

"Now Ni'raisha. You know that there is just not enough room in this house for you, L.T, and a baby. L.T. has the only extra room, and he can barely fit his things in there."

Was she serious? My own mother was really telling me that I could not come and stay with her and I was pregnant with her grandchild. "Alright mom I have to go," I said.

"So where are you going to go?"

"I don't know, Mom!" I yelled. "I don't have anybody!"

"Well why don't you call Jamaal and see if he would let you come and stay with him."

I cut her off. "Okay, Mom I will talk to you later," I said hanging up the phone. I called Jamaal's cell phone but his phone went straight to voicemail. I walked into the bedroom and started packing my bags. There wasn't really any food in the fridge because Ron and I had mostly ordered take out every day. I had grabbed a bag of raisin bread and the half of pack of spring waters that had been in the kitchen. I piled my bags up in the trunk of my car and started car up. Unsure of what to do next I drove around for a few hours.

The sky started to get dark and my gas tank soon was on half. I looked at my phone and thought about calling Jamaal back but decided against it. I had not called nor spoken to Jamaal in months except at Tay's funeral and it wouldn't be fair to call him now because I needed him. I turned my cell phone off to preserve the battery. I was cold, hungry, and tired. With nowhere to go I pulled into the parking lot of a twenty four hour Walmart to get some rest. Grabbing the blanket that I had took from Ron's house out of the back seat, I leaned my seat back and reminisced about my past life until I fell asleep.

When I had awaken in the morning the only thing that was running through my head was that I had to do something. There was no way that I could go another day sleeping in a car and on top of that I was starving and needed to shower. I turned on my cell phone and I had a pending voicemail. It was Ron asking me what was going on and why he was getting my voicemail. He told me that he was going to have his cousin connect him with me later when he calls. I disconnected from my voicemail. Right then was not the time for me to be worried about Ron and what he was going through. Then an idea popped into my head. I searched my call log for Rock's number. I knew that it was wrong but right now I was in desperate need. I had to let my pride go for the time being. I only prayed that he would not blow me off after how rude

I was to him over the phone.

"Yo," he answered the phone.

"Hi Rock?"

"Who is this?"

"This is Ni?"

"How do I know you?" he asked.

"You don't. I called you the other day about Ron."

"Oh this is Ron's shorty. What's up? Did you tell your man what I said?"

"No," I said in a low tone of voice. "I actually haven't had a chance to speak to him."

"Aight. It's obvious you're not calling me about him 'cause you haven't spoken to him so what's your motive?

"Excuse me?" I said.

"I didn't stutter," Rock replied.

"Look I'm calling you because I know at one point you and Ron were close and I know that if you were going through something and you needed Ron he would hold you down," I said not knowing if this was probably not the case.

"Get to the point," he said. "I know I don't know you but if you fucked with Ron in the past then I'm guessing that you can't be too much of a bad guy. I was staying with Ron and I had to leave that house and I really need somewhere to stay for a couple of weeks," I said hoping that by then I could find the courage to contact Jamaal and make things right.

"Oh so you call me? When you was talking to me the other day you was all in love with Ron and shit. You was acting like a nigga was trynna wife you, and I was just fucking with you."

I wanted to curse him out so bad but I held my composure. "It's just that I don't mess around with friends. That's never been my thing," I said thinking of Natty and her phony ass.

"For the last time, I don't fuck with Ron, and he ain't my boy. But let's get straight to the point. Why do you think I should let you come and stay here when your rude ass hung up on me like that?"

In my head, I could see Rock smiling on the other end of the phone. I had to throw myself into survival mode. "Because I won't disappoint you in any way," I said putting on a sexy voice.

Rock laughed. "You think you slick, but I like that response. Aight check it? I'ma let you come stay here for a few weeks but only under one circumstance."

"What's that?" I asked.

"You better not be ugly. If you pull up to my crib looking all crazy and your face ain't what I expect then I'ma tell you to turn around 'cause I don't allow ugly females in my crib," he laughed. "Real talk."

Damn, this dude was acting immature, with that bullshit. "Well I am far from that," I said knowing that I had no worries when it came to my face. Not to toot my own horn but I was one pretty bitch.

"Aight well we will see. You got a pen to take down the address?"

"Go ahead. I'm gonna type it into my GPS," I said starting up the GPS that was built into the dashboard.

"Oh I guess Ron was doing you right, huh?"

"I bought my own car. Thank you." I said.

"Oh okay. I'm sorry," he replied.

Rock gave me the address, and I headed over to what I would call my new home for the next few weeks.

Chapter 15

A month had come and gone and I found myself still staying at Rock's house. I was grateful that he had let me stay there longer than I was supposed to, but I was really ready to go. I still hadn't gotten up the strength to call Jamaal. There was too much that I would have to tell him regarding my situation and I just wasn't ready for that. From day one when I arrived at Rock's house he was sure to let me know how I would show my appreciation to him for what he was doing for me. He would give me a place to lay my head, feed me, and assist me with clothes and gas money to get back and forth to my doctor's appointments. In return I would have to satisfy him sexually, physically and orally. The first time I had had sex with Ron, I tried to make him put on a condom, but he refused. The one thing that I was not going to do was tell him that I was infected with H.I.V.; it was embarrassing enough for me just knowing that I had it. If I had told Rock, he might have kicked my ass out without thinking twice, and if I had told him now he probably would kill my ass so I was just going to have to keep quiet. An unknown number had called me the night that I arrived at Rock's house. I assumed it was Ron, but Rock had forbidden me to talk to him as long as I was in his household. I refused to answer afraid of being caught and thrown out into the streets and this time I would be sleeping in my car permanently. Staying with Rock allowed me to look physically healthy, clean and presentable when I went to visit L.T. Rock also paid my cell phone bill because he didn't want me using his phone but at the same time he understood that I had a child that I needed to stay in contact with. Although Rock was an asshole, I had to give him credit for taking that into consideration.

I had been asleep in Rock's bedroom when I awoke to a loud bang. There was a bunch of yelling coming from the kitchen. I jumped up out of the bed and walked into the kitchen to see what was going on. Rock had been standing over one of his boys, kicking him in his back. There were cards all over the floor, and drinks were spilled everywhere. Rock's other boys just sat there and watched I knew I had to do something before he killed the dude.

"Rock, what are you doing! Stop it!"

Rock stopped kicking him and turned around. "Yo go back in the fucking room!"

I looked down at the guy. His mouth was full of blood, and he lied there helplessly.

"Leave him alone Rock! Just let him go before the neighbors hear all of this noise and call the cops!" I said knowing that I did not need another repeat of Ron's house. I would have thought that Rock would have been smarter than that considering his choice of work.

Rock looked down at his boy on the floor. "Get the fuck out of my house," he said with sweat dripping down his face. He looked over at me as if he had wanted to do to me what he had just done to him. I took that as my cue to leave his presence and so I made my way back into his bedroom. Rock was showing his company out, and I was just grateful that I could finally rest peacefully. The only time I got rest was when he was in the streets hustling, and that was rarely because he had little niggas out there doing it for him. In the time that I had been staying with Rock, there had barely been one day that he did not have company over. They would drink and play blackjack into the wee hours of the morning.

Rock appeared at the bedroom door with his eyebrows lowered and his lips pressed tightly together. "Bitch, who the fuck do you think you are?" he said as he came toward me. He grabbed me by my neck. This is my fucking house! You don't run shit in here! You bum ass broke, bitch! I'm doing you're sorry ass a favor by allowing you to stay here! Don't ever do that bullshit again, you hear me!"

I nodded.

Rock released his grip around my neck. "If you ever get involved in my business again, you will find yourself out there on the streets pregnant or not," he said as he turned and walked out of the room slamming the door behind him. He quickly swung the door back open. "I'm running to grab me something to eat. Just make sure that your ass is laying in that living room chair by the time I get back," he said closing the door again behind him. I leaned up against the headboard as tears formed in my eyes. I knew that I had been in desperate mode, but living with Rock was no longer an option for me. I was tired of being treated like I was an animal and being forced into doing sexual favors to continue to stay with him. I really needed to make things right with Jamaal, but I wasn't ready to let him know exactly how bad I had been doing. I looked at the time on the cable box in the bedroom. It read 10:22. I grabbed my cell phone off of the nightstand and pressed speed dial to call Jamaal.

"Hello," Jamaal answered.

"Hi Jamaal," I said in a low tone.

"What's up, Ni? I hadn't heard from you since the invite that I extended to you at Tay's funeral."

"Yeah I know. This baby just has me really worn out all the time."

"I bet you're getting big," Jamaal said.

"Yes I'm getting there."

"So what's up, Ni? I know you didn't just call me to say hello, so there must be something on your mind."

"Umm, actually I was thinking maybe we can get together and grab something to eat whenever you are available. I have something that I need to talk to you about."

"What do you need to talk to me about?"

"I'd rather talk to you in person, if that's okay."

"Okay cool. How's Friday? Jamaal asked.

"Friday is fine with me."

"Did you want me to grab L.T. from your mom's house so that he can come out with us?"

"No. actually I would rather it be just me and you. What I have to talk to you about is really important, and I don't think that it would be appropriate for L.T. to be present during this conversation"

"Alright, well where did you want to meet at?" Jamaal asked.

"Applebee's is fine. I've been craving some of those ribs anyway," I said laughing.

Jamaal chuckled. "I can be there at about 7:30, is that cool?"

"Yeah. That works for me."

"So I will see you Friday, Ni."

"Okay," I said. "Then it's a date."

"I wouldn't say all that," Jamaal joked.

"Goodbye Jamaal."

"Aight," he said.

After hanging up the phone, I really felt so much regret for everything that I had done to him. I missed all of the laughs we shared together and most of all being in a relationship with someone that I loved and he loved me right back. I grabbed a pillow off the bed. I walked over to Rock's closet to grab a blanket and I made my way to what would be my bed for the night.

When Friday came, I was so relieved to get out of Rock's house for a bit. I have not left his house since I had gotten there unless it was for a doctor's appointment or I had gone by my mom's house to see L.T., which was very rarely. Rock had warned me that I better use any gas money he had given me wisely because I was not his baby's momma, and he was not going to be supporting my every need. I wasn't sure how he had expected $10 a week to take me to a doctor's appointment and to visit my child. That was all the more reason why I had dipped in his stash in his shoebox a couple of times. Lucky for me, his ass was always so high and drunk that he never noticed. The shoebox was what he referred to as his change box because he kept his chump change in there. He would go in there and get a few dollars out if he wanted to grab something to eat or something to drink, so he probably could care less about the money in there just as long as it wasn't his big money.

When I arrived at Applebee's, Jamaal had already been parked sitting in his car. I pulled up on the side of him. Jamaal got out of his car and made his way to the driver side of my car.

"Hey pretty lady," he said opening the door for me.

I smiled, "How are you?"

"I'm good and you?" he said glancing down at my stomach.

"I'm managing."

"Come on and let's get you something to eat. I know you're hungry," Jamaal said jokingly.

"Oh be quiet," I said as I shoved him lightly.

He held the door for me as we made our way inside. Damn, how I missed those days. Ron would barely take me anywhere more like hold a door open for me, and I was just Rock's sex toy so the only people that knew about me were his few boys that came over. I wasn't allowed to hang around his company so the only time they would see me was if I went to the bathroom or in the kitchen to grab something. Rock had forbidden me from being around his company.

Jamaal pulled the chair out for me to sit down. "Thanks," I said. But you do know that I'm pregnant, not handicapped right?"

"Yeah I know, but I'm just trying to be a gentlemen."

Looking into Jamaal's sexy ass hazel eyes just made me want to rewind time. I smiled. "I'm happy to know that you still have it in you."

"Ain't nothing change, I'm still the same Jamaal."

The waitress came to our table to take our orders and then walked off to get our drinks.

So, what did you want to talk to me about Ni?"

"Can we at least get our food first?" I said knowing that Jamaal probably wouldn't be hungry after hearing what I had to say.

"Aight calm down. That pregnancy got you acting all evil." He laughed.

"I am not acting evil."

"You still have the most beautiful smile," Jamaal said.

"Thank you and you still have the most sexy eyes that I have ever seen."

"Oh I know," Jamaal said. "Ni?"

"What's up?"

"I have really been going through a lot since we separated. I hate the way we ended things." I nodded. "I know that we both messed up but I think that if we had just sat down and talked about it then maybe we would still be together. I'm thinking about selling the house."

"Why would you do that?" I asked.

"I'm trying to cut down on some expenses and I figured that I could start by selling the house. I mean it's only me in that big house, and since it doesn't look like you and L.T. are ever coming back I figured I might as well downgrade."

After hearing that I so badly wanted to just tell Jamaal that I wanted to come home. Little did he know that I was living in hell and him saying that let me know that he did want us to come back. I doubted that he would feel this way in the next half hour to come. Jamaal and I enjoyed dinner. We practically joked and laughed the whole time and I could definitely tell that the love was still there.

"So Ni, can I ask you a question?"

"Sure."

"Who do you stay with?"

"Who do you think I stay with?"

"Well I know it's not homeboy 'cause I heard he got knocked. Come on now Ni, you know the streets talk."

I knew the streets talked, but Jamaal rarely hung with dudes, so I started to wonder whether he really got his information from the streets or my mom. I cleared my throat. "I'm staying with a friend."

"Guy or female?" he asked.

I couldn't tell Jamaal the truth. I didn't want to hurt him more than I had already. "A female friend of mine from my old job. I'm actually trying to get on my feet so I can find a place."

"Oh okay. Well you know you're always welcome to come and stay with me if you should need to."

"Yes, I know," I said. Deep down inside I was so happy to hear Jamaal say that. "I will let you know if I can't come up with something."

"Alright, so now what is it that you had wanted to talk to me about?"

Our conversation had been going so good, and I didn't want to ruin the moment. I had to do some quick thinking. There was no way that I was going to kill the mood with bad news. "I was wondering if you would like to choose the baby's name."

"Me?" Jamaal said pointing to himself.

"Yes you silly," I said.

"Damn. I thought you'd never ask."

"Is that a yes?"

"Of course."

"Alright and don't be trying come up with no crazy names like Mercedes or Miracle," I joked.

"Nah I was actually thinking Alize.'" I looked over at Jamaal with a serious face. He laughed. "I'm joking. You know that I am more than capable of picking a good name right?" "Yeah I trust you."

Jamaal walked me to my car and opened the door for me. "Can I get a hug?" he asked.

I gave him a tight hug. After letting go he put his hand on my stomach. "You're daddy's little girl, and I don't care what nobody say."

I smiled and got into my car.

"So when can we do this again?"

"That's up to you." I replied.

"How does next weekend sound? And we can bring L.T. with us this time. Maybe we can do dinner and a movie."

"That sounds good," I said. "I'll talk to you soon." Jamaal kissed me on my cheek and walked off.

When I arrived at Rock's house his car had not been outside and all of the lights were out. I asked him earlier if he had plans on going anywhere because I was going out and I had no key to his apartment to get in. I called his cell phone and got his voicemail. I texted him and asked him what time he would be home and that I was outside waiting to get inside, but he never responded. I laid my seat back figuring I might as well get comfortable. An hour and a half later, Rock pulled up into the driveway blasting his music. "Thank God," I said to myself as I leaned my chair up and grabbed my bag out of the passenger seat. Rock unlocked the door and went inside of the house without even acknowledging me. I walked into the house behind Rock and went right into the bathroom. Sitting in that car for damn near two hours had me feeling like my bladder was going to explode. Rock was such an idiot and I could only hope that Jamaal would ask me and L.T. to come back home soon and this time I would not refuse his offer.

When I was leaving the bathroom, as I opened the door Rock was standing at the door. "Where did you go tonight?"

I didn't want to piss him off. "I went to my mom's house to have dinner with my little man. I told you that I was going to be stepping out earlier."

"You better not had been out there doing nothing other than what you telling me or you gonna find yourself out on the streets."

I rolled my eyes and brushed past Rock into the living room. I grabbed the blanket off of the edge of the couch so that I could lay down.

"What are you sleeping in the living room for? Go take your clothes off and get in the bed," he said. I knew exactly what that meant.

I had to hurry up get away from Rock before he found out that I was H.I.V positive and tried to kill my ass. I didn't fully blame myself for having unprotected sex with him because he was the one that refused to put on a condom no matter how much I insisted.

Thursday night had arrived, and I was so excited for Friday to come so that I can spend the day with Jamaal and L.T. I couldn't sleep because Rock and his company were up drinking, gambling, and making noise. I appreciated the fact that he allowed me to stay there, but he had no consideration for me pregnant or not. I picked up my phone to text Jamaal. I texted him letting him know that I had gone to my doctor's appointment earlier that day and my doctor said that the baby was about three pounds five ounces and she was doing well. He replied that he was happy to hear that and that he was really looking forward to seeing me and L.T. on Friday. If he only knew that I was looking forward to Friday more than him. After texting back and forth with Jamaal, I was in much of a better mood. I rolled over and thought about memorable moments with him until I fell asleep.

"Can I have some of your ice cream?" Jamaal asked as he smiled at me.

"Dad, you can have some of mine," L.T. offered.

"No I don't want any chocolate. "Mommy has strawberry and I want some," he said opening his mouth.

I scooped up a scoop of my ice cream and shoved it in his mouth. L.T. started laughing. "Okay so that's how you gonna do me, huh?" Jamaal said with ice cream all over his lips. I laughed. "It's cool," I will get you back he said smiling and reaching for a napkin.

"Whatever Jamaal."

Jamaal looked over at L.T. "What do you think about you and mommy moving back home?"

I looked at Jamaal in shock.

"Really!" L.T. yelled.

"Yes," he said. "Right Ni?" He looked over at me. "Uh huh," I replied as I looked over at L.T.

"Thank God because I love grandma, but there is really not much to do at her house," L.T. said. "I don't mind spending a weekend over there, but every day is at bit too much."

We all laughed. "Well you don't have to worry about that anymore, Jamaal said.

On the way out, I told L.T. to walk ahead of us. "So did you really want us to come back home?" I said to Jamaal.

"Of course I do, Ni. I just really wanna try and make it work this time around. This nigga is in jail, so even if he is the father, I'm not going to leave you for dead."

A tear ran down my cheek. "Thank you so much," I said kissing him on the lips.

"Now when are you going come home?"

"When do you want me to come home?"

"You can come tonight if you want to. I can go with you to get your things from your friend's house if you want me to."

"Well I don't have much, so why don't you go and grab L.T's things from my mom's house and I will grab my things?"

"Are you sure? I don't want you hurting yourself trying to carry nothing."

"I'm sure, Jamaal."

"Alright. Call me when you are on your way to the house."

"Okay," I said. "I will see you in a few," I said to L.T. as he got into the passenger side of Jamaal's car.

I got into my car and took a deep breath. I was relieved. I would no longer have to deal with the bullshit from Rock, and I would finally be able to have my family back. The only problem with leaving was that I would have to sneak past Rock to do it. I wasn't sure if he would be okay with me leaving or if he would react to it but one thing was for sure, I was not going to take a chance. When I got to the house, Rock's car was in the driveway. I was thankful that he wasn't trying to pull the same thing that he had pulled the week before. I knocked on the door, and Rock answered. He opened the door and went to sitting back on the living room chair watching TV I walked past the couch.

"Where you going?" he asked.

"In the room to change," I said.

I didn't know why he felt the need to know my every move, but at this point I could care less 'cause as soon as his ass went to sleep, I was out of there. I walked into the room and grabbed my two tote bags out of his closet and started stuffing them with my clothes. Whatever couldn't fit would just have to stay. I heard footsteps, and I kicked the bags under his bed. Rock came walking in the room as I started removing my shirt.

"Come here," he signaled for me to come closer. I walked over to him, and he began pulling my pants down. Rock laid me down on the bed and started kissing me when his cell phone rang. "Hold up," he said as he reached in his pocket to grab it. "Yo," he said answering the phone. "Word?" he said as he walked out of the room.

I exhaled.

Rock walked back into room. "Stay just like that," he referred to me being naked. "I gotta handle some business real quick; I'll be right back. "Okay," I said nodding. As soon as I heard Rock's car pull away, I jumped up and threw on my clothes. I kneeled down to grab my bags from under the bed and finished packing as much as I can fit in the bags. I rushed out closing the door behind me and made my way to Jamaal's house. I called Jamaal to let him know that I was on my way over and then I turned my radio up and started bumping Keyshia Cole's sent from heaven. If felt so good to be going home to my man.

Chapter 16

Living with Jamaal had been such a big difference from staying with Ron. I changed my cell phone number to avoid any contact from Ron or Rock. The last thing I needed was one of them to contact me and bring drama back into what Jamaal and I were trying to fix. I had been a month and a half away from my due date, and he had catered to my every need without thinking twice. He rubbed my stomach and my swollen feet. Jamaal would go to work and come straight home to be with L.T. and I. The only issue that still remained was that I had still not told Jamaal my secret. I was able to keep him from attending my doctor's appointments because I had encouraged him to go to work because we needed all of the money we could get with the new baby coming. Jamaal had agreed but said that during the last month he would be attending every weekly appointment with me regardless of what I said. My doctor advised me at my last appointment that my weekly visit would start the following week. I couldn't lie to Jamaal about my appointments. After all that he had done for me it would be selfish and unfair of me to deceive him once again. I had to make him aware of what was taking place with me and what the medicines that I had told him was for my blood pressure were really for. I knew that this could either make or break us but this was something that I had to do and get it over with once and for all.

"Baby!" Jamaal yelled upstairs to me.

"I'm in the bed!" I yelled back.

Jamaal came walking upstairs with a vase full of roses. "Look what I got you," he said smiling.

"Aww, Jamaal you didn't have to do that."

"I know, but I wanted to."

"Thanks," I said kissing him on the lips.

"Where's L.T?" Jamaal asked.

"He's in room studying for a big test."

"That's my boy," he said.

"Starting next week I will be going to the doctor's weekly now that I am a month and a half away from my due date," I said.

"Cool. I finally get to go with you. When is your appointment next week?"

"It's Tuesday at 8:30."

"I will just go in to work late and stay a little late."

"That works for me," I said with a fake smile on my face. There was no way Jamaal was not going to attend my last few appointments so if there was any better time to tell him it would have to be this weekend.

"Jamaal?"

"Yes baby?" he said as he leaned over and kissed my belly.

"I was thinking that maybe this weekend we could get some alone time at home. Just you and I and I will cook you a nice dinner."

"I'm cool with that. So when did you wanna do this Friday or Saturday?"

"How's Saturday? I was hoping that you, me, and L.T. can maybe go to the movies on Friday and then out for some ice cream."

"You been doing a lot of thinking since you pregnant," Jamaal joked.

I smiled. "I'm just playing with you, baby. So I guess Saturday works. Be sure to give your mom a call and let her know that I'm gonna be dropping L.T. off Saturday. It will probably be around three 'cause I promised him that I would buy him a pair of sneakers and then I was gonna take him to GameStop to pick up that NBA2k11 that he wanted."

"Okay," I said.

"Cool."

"So I will give her a call sometime tomorrow. Are you hungry?" I asked.

"Only for you," Jamaal said kissing me on my neck.

I laughed. "I put your plate in the microwave for you now go ahead and eat it before I eat it for you. You know I'm eating for two."

Jamaal stood up off of the bed. "Well in that case I better go ahead and eat. You need anything from downstairs?"

"No I'm okay," I said.

"Alright then suit yourself," he said as he headed down the stairs.

Saturday had seemed to come faster than usual. I guess that I was hoping that the days would go by slow to avoid having to break the news to Jamaal but it didn't work in my favor. I got up out of the bed and headed downstairs to make coffee and some breakfast before Jamaal and L.T. headed out.

I was fixing everyone's plate when Jamaal came walking downstairs. "Good morning, baby."

"Good morning," I replied. "How did you sleep?"

"I slept okay, and how about you and the little one?"

"Could be better? You want some coffee?"

"Yeah. I'll take a cup," Jamaal said. He yelled for L.T. to come downstairs and eat.

L.T. came running down the stairs excited.

"Hey. You know we don't run in this house," Jamaal said.

"Sorry dad."

"What are you all excited about anyways?" I asked him. "

Dad's taking me to get a new video game today! I can't wait!"

"If I catch you running down the steps again, your behind can kiss that game goodbye," I said.

"I promise I won't do it again mom," L.T. said as he sat at the kitchen table.

"Alright now, come on and hurry up and eat so that we can get a move on it."

"So where are you and mom going today that ya'll just wanna drop me off to grandma's house?"

"Somewhere you're not," Jamaal joked. "Now eat your food before you find yourself going straight from here to your grandmother's."

L.T. picked up his fork and starting eating. I looked at both of them and smile. They were the two most important men in my life, and I knew that there was no one else that I could've been happier with.

I was in the kitchen making dinner before Jamaal got home. I set the table up with a few candles that I had grabbed from the store earlier when I ran out to grab my prescription refill. My phone rang, and it was Jamaal.

"Hey babe," I answered.

"Hey. I'm about to take L.T. to grab some ice cream and then I'm gonna drop him to your mom's house. I should be there in about an hour."

"Alright. Take your time," I said knowing that I needed just a little more time to set the mood. I was hoping that Jamaal would really forgive me for what I had done to him and I knew that having this conversation would definitely turn the mood sour but if this turned out to be the last day that I ever got to spend with him, then I definitely wanted to make sure it was special.

Jamaal walked in the house with a surprised look on his face. "Wow. You got a red light special going on here and I get steak for dinner?" he said.

I walked over to him and kissed him. "Only for you," I said smiling. "Now have a seat."

Jamaal sat down. I poured him a glass of wine and set it next to his plate. If he drank enough before I was able to tell him then maybe it would lighten the load. Jamaal took a sip of the wine.

"Did you and L.T. enjoy your day out?"

"Yeah but you know L.T. is a slick dude. We went to get one game and came out with two."

I laughed. "He knows that he can only pull that mess with you 'cause I ain't having it."

"Yeah. I know. I talked to your mom for a few minutes when I got there."

"What was she talking about?"

"She was just asking how things were going with us, and she hopes that I can forgive you so that we can move forward. I told her I've already forgiven you." Jamaal chuckled.

I set my fork down and put my head down.

"What's wrong with you?" Jamaal said taking a bite of his steak.

"Jamaal, there is something that I have to tell you, and I know right now it may upset, you but I hope that you will forgive me so that we can try and work through this."

Jamaal set his fork down. "Work through what, Ni?"

I stayed quiet.

"Ni what are you talking about? What - is there somebody else that might be the father of the baby besides me and the other dude?"

"No," I said shaking my head.

"Alright Ni, look. We both been through enough with each other already so if we are going work this out then we need to be honest with each other."

"I know."

"Then stop procrastinating and just tell me what you need to tell me."

I could tell that Jamaal was growing impatient with me so I just came out with it. "Jamaal, I tested positive for H.I.V."

"What!" Jamaal yelled standing up from the table.

"I'm sorry, Jamaal, I've been wanting to tell you so bad. The medicine that I told you that I was taking for high blood pressure-"

Jamaal interrupted. "You fucking lied, didn't you! So you're telling me that there is a chance that I'm sick, too!"

I stood up from the table and flipped on the kitchen light switch. "I'm sorry! I swear to God I am! I never meant to hurt you, Jamaal!" I started crying.

"How long have you known, huh? You know what, it doesn't even fucking matter! You fucking put me in this position 'cause you wanted to go out and sleep with some random dude now I'ma have to live with this shit!"

I couldn't deny that I was wrong for what I did, but I couldn't help but be offended. "The nerve of you to talk about me cheating when you fucked my best friend!"

"I fucked Natty, but I made sure I used a condom and maybe if you would've practiced safe sex then we wouldn't be in this predicament!"

Jamaal was right. There was nothing else that I could say to defend myself. Nothing could justify the pain that I had caused him by allowing this to happen.

Jamaal turned around and punched a hole in the kitchen wall.

"Jamaal!" I yelled.

"Get your shit and get the fuck out of my house now!" he said.

"Jamaal please! Can I just talk to you?"

"Get the fuck out!" Jamaal said pointing toward the living room.

"Fine. I'm going to put some clothes on and I will be out of your damn house, but the fact that I am pregnant still remains!"

"What the fuck does it matter, huh? Thanks to you and your stupid ass decisions, the fucking baby might be born with it! And if that is the case I swear to God, Ni, I will take your irresponsible ass to court for custody if it is mine! If it's not my baby then you're on your fucking own 'cause I don't want shit to do with you and I want you to stay the fuck away from me until you have that baby and we have the blood work done!"

"Jamaal, do you hear what you are saying right now! Are you really willing to just kick me out the on the streets pregnant and knowing that I have nowhere else to go!"

Jamaal took a deep breath and exhaled "Get your things and get out, Ni." I looked Jamaal in his eyes, and I could see that he was upset and hurt at the same time. I made my way upstairs to change my clothes. I grabbed my tote bag so that I could pack my things, but I decided against it. I didn't think that I would need it where I was going. All that I could think about was Jamaal, L.T, and the baby. I fucked up, and I wasn't worthy of being a wife or a mother. When I got dressed and made my way back downstairs, Jamaal was in the living room pacing back and forth. I opened up the front door and turned around in hopes that I could get Jamaal's attention, but he refused to even look at me.

"I'm sorry," I said and I walked out closing the door behind me.

As I drove away in my car, flashbacks of everything that had taken place in my life had come into play. I started to cry again only this time I couldn't stop. I couldn't believe this was my life. A life that was once perfect had now become a nightmare. I had lost my best friend and my fiancé. I practically poisoned the life that was inside of me, and L.T. wasn't even aware of my condition. My supposedly friend had been sleeping with my fiancé. I was pregnant and didn't even know who my child's father was and either way both of them were gone. I had been forced into sexually pleasuring my potential baby father's ex-friend just to keep a roof over my head and food in my mouth. My own mother who birthed me wouldn't even allow me to stay in her home in a time of need I was H.I.V positive, and who the hell knew when I was going to die. I had nothing, no one, and nowhere to go. This had to be the end for me. I wiped my eyes and continued to drive until I reached the off ramp on I-95. Knowingly driving the wrong way, I drove up the ramp, pushing the gas pedal as far down as it would go. I closed my eyes and continued to drive as fast as my car would allow me. Horns were honking, but I never opened my eyes, and I didn't stop. Once again thoughts began to cloud my head. Thoughts of what I had, who I was, and who I had become. I could no longer live with myself. Everything that I had worked so hard for had been taking from me and there was no way that I was going to bring my baby into the world to have Jamaal just take her from me. I couldn't bring a child with H.I.V into such a cruel world. This was not my baby's fault, and I refused to let her suffer the consequences of my actions. I was tired of being known as the good girl gone bad. I removed my hands from the steering wheel. Physically, I didn't know where I was going but one thing was for sure, I no longer desired to remain here on earth.

About the Author

Shaneschia Kay was born and raised in Bridgeport, Connecticut. No stranger to the atrocities that come along with living in poverty stricken area, Shaneschia managed to survive in an area filled with frequent drug dealing, robberies and killings. Staying strong, Shaneschia's writing has been strongly influenced by her experiences in such an environment.

At the age of 12, Shaneschia found that she had a passion for writing. On rainy days, as the sound of water pouring down could be compared to that of hammers hitting the ground with clouds covering the bright sun, Shaneschia would grab her notebook, lay down on her bed, and write poetry for hours.

In high school after winning an award at a poetry contest, Shaneschia was convinced that she could pursue writing. She found that anything, if interesting enough, motivated her to write, something that still holds true to this day. Currently pursuing a bachelor's degree in Healthcare Administration, Shaneschia continues to write not only because she wants

to, but also because her passion doesn't allow

her a choice. Writing is a love that she wishes

to pass on to her readers.

Visit The Official Author's Website
For More Information

Follow on Facebook, BurstOut, Twitter,
Instagram, & Youtube